"Do you believe in we
Cecile asked

Luke frowned. "Define what you mean."

"The feeling that there's something in the air at
weddings. Something that makes people do
things they shouldn't."

He nodded. "I know what you're talking about.
From the first moment I saw you, I wasn't
settling for anything less. Why else would I leave
when you did?" He'd moved toward her, almost
as close as he'd been during their first slow
dance.

She'd been seduced before, but never like this.
Luke was out of her league. Her body hummed.
"You don't make anything easy, do you?"

"Never." He ran a finger down her bare arm.
"I get what I want, Cecile. Always have, always
will."

"And what do you want?" she said, her breath
lodging in her throat as she waited for his reply.

"You." His tone was forceful and determined. A
thrill shot through her. "And I definitely want
this."

With that, he lowered his mouth and kissed her.

Dear Reader,

I love weddings and wedding magic. This past April and July, I had a chance to attend two weddings, each for one of my work colleagues. Watching them say their vows and seeing how much love existed between them gave me such a happy feeling. Weddings are that one moment in time when everything is magic, when the future is unlimited. I have no doubt that each of my colleagues will live happily ever after.

For Cecile, though, weddings are a reminder that her future hasn't quite turned out as she envisioned it. When her best friend announces her own impending nuptials, Cecile worries that life might be passing her by. Determined to at least have a grand passion, Cecile lets the magic sweep her into the arms of Luke Shaw. There's just one little problem. When she begins her new dream job, Cecile learns that Luke is her boss—and her company has a "no fraternization" policy. So what's a girl going to do to win her man? Turn the pages and find out!

I hope you enjoy *The Wedding Secret*, the second book in my AMERICAN BEAUTIES miniseries. Please join me when Tori's story, *Nine Months' Notice*, concludes the series in April 2007.

Until then, enjoy the romance and feel free to drop me an e-mail at michele@micheledunaway.com. Happy reading.

All the best,

Michele Dunaway

The Wedding Secret
MICHELE DUNAWAY

HARLEQUIN®

TORONTO • NEW YORK • LONDON
AMSTERDAM • PARIS • SYDNEY • HAMBURG
STOCKHOLM • ATHENS • TOKYO • MILAN • MADRID
PRAGUE • WARSAW • BUDAPEST • AUCKLAND

ISBN-13: 978-0-373-75148-8
ISBN-10:   0-373-75148-6

THE WEDDING SECRET

ABOUT THE AUTHOR

In first grade, Michele Dunaway wanted to be a teacher when she grew up, and by second grade she wanted to be an author. By third grade, she was determined to be both, and before her high school class reunion, she'd succeeded. In addition to writing romance, Michele is a nationally recognized high school English and journalism educator. Born and raised in a west county suburb of St. Louis, Michele has traveled extensively, with the cities and places she's visited often becoming settings for her stories. Described as a woman who does too much but doesn't know how to stop, Michele gardens five acres in her spare time and shares her life with two young daughters, six lazy house cats, one dwarf rabbit and two tankfuls of fish.

Michele loves to hear from readers. You can reach her via her Web site, www.micheledunaway.com.

Books byMichele Dunaway

HARLEQUIN AMERICAN ROMANCE

 988—THE PLAYBOY'S PROTÉGÉE
1008—ABOUT LAST NIGHT...
1044—UNWRAPPING MR. WRIGHT
1056—EMERGENCY ENGAGEMENT
1100—LEGALLY TENDER
1116—CAPTURING THE COP
1127—THE MARRIAGE CAMPAIGN*

*American Beauties

For Oprah Winfrey, thanks for being a voice of the people. You have made a positive difference in the lives of so many. And to Jennifer Green, thanks for being such a terrific editor who's willing to push me where I need it.

Chapter One

He was the man she was fated to walk down the aisle with, a man she barely knew. As Cecile Duletsky took a steadying breath, she told herself she would not kill her sister.

At least not today, her wedding day.

Okay, if Cecile were honest, it wasn't *exactly* her younger sister's fault that in less than one hour Cecile would march down the long, white-runner-covered aisle of St. Donovan's Church on the arm of Luke Shaw, a man hotter than a summer day. A man who, when Cecile had first spoken to him last night during the rehearsal dinner, had made her feel undressed with just the twinkle of his blue eyes.

The way Cecile figured it, she should have been allowed to walk down the aisle by herself, as she had at any other wedding she'd been in. But no, someone higher up on her sister's wedding party chain of command had overruled Cecile in the interest of making the exceedingly long July ceremony all of two tiny minutes shorter.

Cecile figured the same higher-up had to have picked out the horrifying purple bridesmaid dress she was wearing. Her sister, Elizabeth, couldn't have become this tasteless in the eleven years the two sisters had been apart. Even the most uneducated fashionista would have known better.

But the hideously oversize bow settling directly over Cecile's bosom proved otherwise, especially as it smashed all of her assets into oblivion instead of enhancing them. The dress added ten pounds to Cecile's figure—the same ten that a daily workout regime assured never touched her slim hips.

The reality was that Elizabeth Duletsky's bridal party looked like grapes gone sour.

At least Cecile's long strawberry-blond hair was up, lifted and twisted just this morning into a high chignon that gave her the appearance of a long swanlike neck.

She'd refused to let the makeup artist hired for the occasion touch her face, opting instead to do her own makeup. Considering the blatant amount of kohl eyeliner on some of the bridesmaids, Cecile knew she'd made a wise choice. Her skin was pale and creamy, a blessing of Irish genetics somewhere in her very mixed lineage. She had green eyes—toss a green costume on her and she could pass for a cute leprechaun. She often had, twice a year—once for St. Patrick's Day and the other for Halloween.

"So are you nervous?" some silly bridesmaid tittered at Cecile's sister. The dark-headed one in the family, Elizabeth sipped her mimosa before shaking her head and replying, "No."

Cecile stood and stepped back from the scene unfolding in the church's anteroom. Unlike the rest of the bridesmaids, who were also all married, Cecile wasn't partaking in the champagne-and-orange-juice concoction the wedding coordinator had provided to settle any last-minute bridal party jitters. Besides, Cecile had always thought it wiser to drink *after* the event. Speaking of said event…

She glanced at her bare left wrist and sighed. No matter how pretty, she'd been told her Cartier watch didn't fit the wedding's dress code and so her favorite accessory was tucked away in her purse. Hopefully it was almost time for the evening nuptials to begin.

The bridal party had been secluded for the last hour, left to the mimosas and their own devices. Of course, the mother of the bride, the mother of the groom and the wedding coordinator and her army of assistants had kept popping in to make final adjustments to some imaginary something.

Cecile's parents, especially her mother, Clarann, were in heaven. Even the groom's family was thrilled. And each family had spent a small fortune for the nuptials to be absolutely perfect.

As for Cecile, she would have been satisfied watching the blessed event from a safe spot in a pew. But the wedding coordinator had insisted on Cecile's presence in the wedding party, saying it would be a major faux pas if the elder sister were left out.

So Cecile had been tossed into the proverbial mix, fitted for a purple dress and surrounded by five additional attendants, all friends of Elizabeth from her college days at Northwestern University. Elizabeth's best friend had garnered maid of honor duties, but Cecile really hadn't minded.

Heck, given her choice, if Cecile ever found the right guy, she'd take the money her parents were spending, elope and buy a sports car. Something cherry-red with a convertible top.

Cecile paced the small room, sending perfunctory smiles to anyone who happened to glance her way. All this money for one day seemed so…overblown.

Deep down she was happy for her sister, and Cecile berated herself as guilt crept in. Twenty-nine was too young to be this cynical, but she'd resigned herself.

She'd long ago pledged to have it all—she and her three friends Lisa, Tori and Joann had made a champagne pact upon graduation. But Cecile had quickly thrown off the naiveté and blinders of college. Over eight years later, Cecile hadn't reached the top and hadn't found the man of her dreams—most of them had been duds.

Her sister's nuptials were showing how flawed Cecile was, and she didn't like the exposure. Despite their not being close, Elizabeth was her sister, and today of all days Cecile should be consumed with overwhelming joy. But instead she was morbidly considering how her own life had gone astray.

To her disgust, she'd become like one of the guests on the talk shows she produced: "My sister married before me and I'm miserable." "My sister has it all and I don't." "My only consolation is that the dress is ugly!"

She did have to admit she was slightly jealous of Elizabeth and Devon, as well. Anyone could look at them and see how much they loved each other. Theirs was a marriage that everyone knew would last. Maybe that was what was putting Cecile into a slight funk, keeping her from being ecstatic that her little sister had found the man of her dreams.

Cecile couldn't even keep her live-in boyfriend, Eric, from straying. She'd been traveling and producing morning-show segments and had come home early one day to find him and another woman in her bedroom. It still bothered her that she could have misjudged their relationship so much.

Weddings also reminded Cecile that life was passing her by—that while perhaps she would have the great career she'd vowed to have, she might not necessarily have a man to go with it. Jaded by a string of wrong turns, she'd preferred relationships with a bunch of temporary, superficial Mr. Right Nows. Surface emotions were easier to handle, and it hurt less when the relationship ended.

Besides, after producing several "My husband cheated with my best friend and she's having his baby" shows, Cecile would rather be alone than become part of the half-the-marriages-fail statistic.

Cecile fingered the purple fabric that reflected the light worse than a cheap shower curtain liner. She and Elizabeth weren't exactly buddies—the five-year age difference between them had meant that Cecile had left for college before her sister had even started high school.

Cecile really did love her sister and wanted to grow closer, perhaps eventually as close as Cecile was to her three best friends, Joann, Lisa and Tori. They'd shared confidences since pledging the same sorority together: Rho Sigma Gamma—the Roses.

Now that Cecile had returned to her hometown of Chicago, maybe she and her sister could forge a real friendship that didn't just involve swapping obligatory Christmas and birthday presents. Maybe they could find some common ground.

Cecile had been gone a while. She'd left home at eighteen for the University of Missouri—Columbia's fabled journalism school—and after graduation she'd been working at a variety of television jobs.

Now she was back home, ready to start her new job as an assistant producer for *The Allegra Montana Show,* meaning she'd be responsible for producing one to two shows per week. While her title read assistant, that only applied to her pay. Aside from the show runner who oversaw all the segment producers, Cecile had the same production responsibilities as everyone else.

Allegra's talk show had been climbing in ratings and popularity for the past three years, especially after a former talk-show host had canceled his show to run for political office. Allegra, who served as executive producer and on-screen talent, had moved into both his vacant studios and his coveted afternoon time slot and never looked back. Her show covered everything from political commentary to celebrity cook-offs.

Chicago was home to many popular talk-show studios, and Cecile's starting date had provided her with just enough time to finish her former job in New York City and cram in her sister's wedding. She'd also managed to find time to rent a Cathedral District apartment which was undergoing some last-minute maintenance. While her stuff had been delivered, Cecile wouldn't occupy the place until Sunday.

At the corner of State Street and Superior, the fifty-two-floor building came complete with a whole-foods store, a pool on the seventh floor and a health club. While Cecile's unit didn't have a lake view, she'd fallen in love with the location, which was only a few blocks west of the Water Tower. She was still almost in the heart of downtown.

Cecile returned her attention to her sister. They were so different, both in looks and temperament. Elizabeth worked for a charity, doing communications work. She planned to work only until her first child, which she would start trying for immediately. Her husband was turning thirty-four in September. An up-and-coming orthopedic surgeon in an already-established practice, Elizabeth and Devon had bought a big house in Barrington a block or two over from both "Grandmas" and started renovations for when the stork arrived.

That was one area of which Cecile wasn't envious. Even though she'd be thirty August fifteenth, no biological clock ticked in her head. Women in their forties had children. Heck, women had children without men. She'd produced a show on the very subject only a few months ago.

"Whose phone is ringing?" someone suddenly asked, jarring Cecile's reverie. The bridesmaids, happily buzzed on mimosas, chimed "Not mine" one after the other.

Cecile blinked. By now everyone was staring at her, and she realized it was her cell phone loudly trilling "Take Me Out to the Ballgame." An avid sports fan, the jingle had been the perfect download.

All the bridesmaids had been given matching purple sequined purses, and Cecile squatted down to remove the phone from the bag resting at her feet. The custom ringtone meant one thing—the caller was one of her three best friends. She glanced at the number. Lisa. A very welcome intrusion.

"Excuse me," Cecile said as she straightened, the floor-length fabric rustling. "I need to take this call. I'll only be a moment."

She ignored the group's speculation and opened the heavy wooden door. The church hallway was cool, and as she stepped onto the marble floor, she could see guests arriving in the church's narthex. Cecile pressed the talk button, catching her former roommate's call before it rolled to voice mail.

"Hey, Lisa, what's up?" Cecile said. "You just saved me from sitting any longer in a room full of tipsy bridesmaids. Please tell me we weren't like that when we were twenty-four."

"I don't think so," Lisa said. "At least not all the time.

But you're busy, so, Cecile, I'll make this quick. You won't believe it, but Mark and I are getting married!"

"Congrats," Cecile said. Her brow wrinkled as the significance of the announcement dawned. Lisa— married? Cecile had to admit she was stunned. They'd always joked that Lisa would be the last one wed. Had she really said *married?* Was she...?

"And, no, I'm not pregnant," Lisa said, laughing as if anticipating the question. "I'm in love."

"Wow. That was fast." Cecile said, catching her breath to hide her shock. Lisa wasn't the impulsive type, and when Cecile had last seen Lisa a few weeks ago during Cecile's layover in St. Louis, Lisa had been wrestling with starting one of those "friends with benefits" relationships with Mark.

So married. Already? No one should get married this fast, unless perhaps they were trying out for a Valentine's Day talk show or a free wedding gown.

"It happens that way," Lisa said as if reading Cecile's thoughts again. "You know what this means, don't you? I'm not going to be the last one married anymore. And since Tori's too busy with Jeff to ever settle down, that means one thing. Cecile, the order's changed. You, my friend, are next."

Cecile frowned. She knew all about the "order." On the night before their sorority initiation, the girls had been camped out in the common room. Dreaming of the future, they'd predicted the order of their marriages. They'd also selected who'd be the maid of honor for whom. Thus, Lisa had stood next to Joann, who'd married right out of college. Cecile would stand next to Lisa. Tori would stand next to Cecile. And Joann would stand next to Tori, making the circle complete.

"I'm hardly next," Cecile said with a disbelieving snort, thrilled for her friend yet cynical about her prediction. "It would take a man for that, and I certainly don't have one of those in the picture at this moment."

"No one?" Lisa said, sounding like a woman in love who wants everyone to be as happy as she. "I guess we really didn't get to talk much about your love life when you were here. But you always have a guy waiting in the wings somewhere. Surely there's someone."

There was always someone, just not *the* one. Cecile wanted that deep emotional connection and refused to settle until she found it. A noise sounded behind her, but Cecile dismissed it. "I wish I could tell you I'm dating someone, but I just relocated. I have a new career. No time."

"I'd just relocated to St. Louis and look what happened to me," Lisa said.

Cecile pointed her foot and touched the tip of her shoe to the floor, her body full of pent-up energy. "Lisa, you know I love you, but no boyfriends are on my radar. Besides, there's always Bob. He's much easier to deal with than love. Much simpler."

"TMI!" Lisa shouted before she began laughing. "Oh, you kill me. I do not want to know if you have a battery-operated boyfriend."

"Don't worry, I don't," Cecile said, smiling. Talking to Lisa always chased away the doldrums, especially as she was easy to tease. "However, if I ever tell you I'm dating Bob, you'll know that my life as I know it is over. Put me on a talk show. I will have given up on men."

"I just said I didn't want to know. Now I know why I stopped being roommates with you. You are way too blunt with information."

Cecile could hear the mirth in Lisa's voice. Funny how she could just pick up and talk to Lisa as if it were yesterday. "Ha-ha. The real reason we split up was because I got a job in New York and had to move away."

"Yeah, be technical," Lisa said, her amusement obvious. "Anyway, I know you're at your sister's wedding so I'll cut this short. Just like we planned all those years ago, I want you to be my maid of honor. It's time."

"Of course you can count on me," Cecile said, warmth tingling her toes. While she might be a little shocked by the sudden turn of events, she knew Lisa better than she knew her own sister. If Lisa had decided Mark Smith was the one, then he was. "You know I'd be honored to stand by your side when you get married." *Even if it means enduring another wedding, another reminder that perhaps my Mr. Right doesn't exist.*

"Thank you. I know it's sudden. But, Cecile, I love him. He's always been the one, even after the fiasco at Joann's reception. We've wasted eight years, and I refuse to wait anymore now that we're finally together. I'll tell you all the details next time I see you—or at least talk to you when you aren't needed elsewhere."

"You'd better," Cecile said automatically. "I think I rate a scoop after everything we've been through."

They'd pledged the sorority together, shared initiation rituals, gossip and dreams. They'd even shared an apartment for a while.

But it was still a bit surreal to imagine Lisa getting married, especially to Mark Smith, a man she'd despised and labeled a playboy. There had to be a show in that: "I'm marrying the man I always thought I hated."

"Look, my sister's wedding is about to start," Cecile told Lisa. "I'll call you later, okay?"

"That's fine. I didn't mean to disturb you, but I wanted you to know first. I still haven't called Tori. She's next."

"Well, go call her. She'll hate you if you don't tell her within a few hours of calling me," Cecile joked.

"I'll call her the moment I hang up. And you go pick up some hunky groomsman. I'm sure he'd be better in bed than Bob any day."

Cecile laughed at that. "I don't know. Bob can be pretty low-maintenance."

"You'll never change. Find someone human. Someone sexy," Lisa insisted.

"He'd have to be much better than that for me to consider it."

"There has to be someone," Lisa persisted. "You're the one who's always telling me to loosen up. Come on," she cajoled, "surely there's one person who might fit the bill?"

"There is. The guy I have to walk down the aisle with. Luke Shaw. Surfer-boy looks. Body to die for. Charisma and class." And that dimple in his cheek had been so tempting, making any woman want to trace it after making love…

Luke was a real flesh-and-blood man, not a fantasy. Still, what would he be like?

"He sounds absolutely scrumptious. Go for it," Lisa said, jolting Cecile back to the present.

"Maybe I will. Maybe I won't," Cecile said. She certainly didn't need to be considering having sex with Luke Shaw, no matter how attractive the guy was. Her focus should be on saying goodbye and getting back to the wedding, not that she wanted to do either. "Right now forget my troubles and consider yourself getting a big hug through the phone. You are very lucky and I'm thrilled for you. Unlike me needing to get through today."

"That bad?" Lisa said, prolonging the conversation one more minute, as they had so often done in the past.

"Oh, yes," Cecile said with a nod. "So before I let you go, promise you'll do me one favor."

"What? You know I'll do anything."

Cecile used her free hand to finger the fabric of her gown. "That's good, because I'm going to send you a photo of this dress. If you care about me, don't make me wear anything this hideous again. I look like a fat purple grape."

Lisa began to laugh, and Cecile realized how much she missed her friend. "I promise not to torture you," Lisa said. "Go survive and be sure to have at least one drink for me. And don't forget to hit on that guy."

"As soon as this thing's over, I'm having at least two. As for hitting on Luke? We'll see. You know I'm trying to turn over a new leaf."

"Start tomorrow afternoon," Lisa joked before saying her goodbyes.

Yes, but starting tomorrow afternoon would sort of defeat the whole purpose of beginning anew. Upon her return to Chicago, Cecile had set three goals. One, excel at her career. Two, become closer with her sister. And three, try to avoid Mr. Right Now and instead find Mr. Right. So no matter how much she might be tempted, she'd decided to hold out for something that at least had potential. New city. New attempt.

Cecile ended the call, closed the phone and turned. She then did a double take and took a much-needed step back.

Luke Shaw hovered about five feet away, as if waiting for her. He gave her a killer smile that made the big, bad wolf seem tame. Damn, but the man did something to her equilibrium. Already her skin heated, as if he'd run a finger down her arm instead of just giving her a smoldering glance.

"I've been looking for you," he said.

Chapter Two

Cecile winced. How long had he been there? How much had he overheard? Had he heard her say she thought he had a body to die for? Had he understood her meaning when she'd said, "Maybe I will"?

If so, he wasn't telling. He stood there and stared at her, a poker facade having fallen into place. Cecile blinked and tried to read him. She'd been having a conversation—a private conversation—involving Bobs and picking up groomsmen.

"Is there something wrong?" Luke asked, that sexy voice of his low and deep. It rumbled over her, sending some foreign sensation to her toes.

He'd overheard her. She was certain of it, especially when that devastatingly handsome smile of his widened suddenly. He was Mr. Charming and he knew it.

But two could play at this game. So like a cat that always landed on her feet, Cecile quickly found her poise. She had a lifetime of experience in handling men like Luke Shaw—they'd come out of the woodwork ever since she'd passed that awkward stage and developed breasts.

"I would say that the only thing wrong is that you've crept up on me. One should be able to have a private conversation in a church, don't you agree?"

He laughed at that, another deep rumble that sounded great. "Sorry if I surprised you, but I was sent to find you. Not my fault or intention to surprise you," Luke said, his big wide hands open in a gesture of mock defense for his loitering.

"So let me guess—someone got all panicky that, instead of indulging in mimosas, I escaped," Cecile said.

"Devon's mother," Luke confirmed. "Although when I was told to find a missing bridesmaid, I wasn't surprised to discover you were the one I was searching for."

"I must have *errant* stamped on my forehead," Cecile said. "I had a phone call I needed to take, of which I'm sure you got quite an earful since you chose to eavesdrop."

Luke shrugged, his countenance not the slightest bit guilty or sheepish. "I will admit to hearing some of it. Good news, I gathered, and some other parts that sounded rather intriguing."

"Yes, I'm sure you were flattered to hear your name," Cecile said. "But I doubt that's anything new. The gist is that I just learned my best friend is getting married and I'm going to be her maid of honor."

"Congratulations," Luke said.

Cecile took a moment to size him up. With her heels, they stood eye to eye, and since she was five foot ten, that made him about six feet. He was trim and his tux fit. Perfectly.

She swallowed and rallied. "As to the other part, Lisa just wanted to know if there were any single men here tonight. I couldn't disappoint her."

"I'm glad I could help out," Luke said, his blue eyes twinkling. "In fact, I happen to agree with you one hundred percent on my attributes. If you'd like, I'd be happy to return the favor and list yours. That is, if Bob won't mind and think you're hitting on me. I'd hate to stop you from turning over a new leaf."

"Believe me, you won't," Cecile said, regaining the upper hand. "Not that I date anyone named Bob. Really, I'm sure we should be getting back."

As if by kismet, Devon's mother approached, her loud "There you both are!" echoing off the walls. "Luke, I send you to find her and you get lost, too!"

"Sorry," Luke said. He bent down and kissed the petite woman's cheek. "Got distracted. Cecile was telling me about Bob."

"Bob? Is he here, at the wedding?" Amanda Pinewood asked.

Luke was a cad, and Cecile resisted the childish urge to stomp on his foot. He had overheard and understood *everything* and he wasn't afraid to tease her with it. As if confirming his rogueness, Luke winked as Cecile sputtered, "Uh, no, Bob's not here."

"Oh, that's good," Amanda said, relieved. "It's time to line up, and you two are not in your proper place."

"Heaven forbid," Luke teased, that wicked smile of

his widening again. Cecile knew that Luke and Devon had grown up as next-door neighbors and buddies. Luke held his arm out to Cecile. "Shall we?"

She'd had to touch him last night at the rehearsal. Then, he'd caused her metabolism to shift into fast-forward, as if she'd just chugged an energy drink. A big believer in chemistry, Cecile wasn't sure what type of pheromones Luke possessed, but he oozed them. Especially now, when they were all directed at her.

But she was Cecile Duletsky, talk-show producer and woman who'd met celebrities on a daily basis when she'd been a talent procurer. She could handle Luke Shaw.

Cecile slipped her bare arm in his, the smooth feel of his tuxedo creating friction against her bare skin. She tried to ignore the immediate heat, but it was near impossible to ignore the presence of the man who walked easily by her side as if he somehow belonged there.

Ushers were working to get the last guests seated so the ceremony could start. Belatedly Cecile remembered her cell phone. She glanced in horror at the silver device still dangling from the strap on her wrist.

"Let me," Luke said, his deep voice close to her ear as he leaned into her. He slid the phone from her wrist, the gesture intimate. Quickly he pressed a few buttons to silence the ringer and then slipped the phone inside his jacket pocket. He grinned. "You can get it from me later."

Later. That word had been loaded.

Wedding magic, Cecile decided. That was all this tickling sensation Luke Shaw incited was, nothing more. She could produce an entire talk-show episode on wedding magic entitled "Wedding secrets—who else shared the night besides the bride and groom?"

While wedding magic wasn't anything tangible, the results often were. For some reason, all the happiness in the air at weddings often led to many singles hooking up. No one wanted to be alone when two people were making a lifetime commitment.

Heck, even Lisa and Mark had shared a passionate kiss in the hallway outside Joann's reception eight years ago. Now they were getting married, proof that wedding magic was real and could lead to something more than one night.

Cecile had arrived solo to Elizabeth's nuptials. She was family and she'd learned long ago that when you were a member of a bridal party, it was often better to attend the official events alone unless you were really serious about some guy.

Luke Shaw was attending stag, as well, according to Elizabeth, who had seen fit to impart the information to Cecile just last night. Her sister had even added that Luke wasn't dating anyone. Cecile hadn't misread her sister's matchmaking attempt and she didn't believe she was currently misreading Luke's not-so-subtle signals that he was interested, especially as he took her arm when the string quartet began the processional music.

"You're starting to fit there," he whispered.

Cecile sucked in her breath and smiled. Yep. Luke was one hot package, and the pendulum of maybe indulging versus maybe not was swinging back and forth. Was she interested in indulging in a little wedding magic? Cecile wasn't one who let the good catches get by without a little taste.

Yet she'd set a goal to stop wasting time on Mr. Man of the Moment, a resolution Lisa had told Cecile to start tomorrow. Luke chose that second to reach over with his free hand, lightly touching the arm she'd looped through his. Heat increased between them and Cecile shifted. Reality was, she knew nothing about him except that he lived in Chicago and he was Devon's best friend. Time to swing the pendulum back the other direction, toward "better not."

"Ready?" Luke arched a blond brow in her direction, and Cecile tried not to shiver with desire. She doubted she'd ever be prepared to totally take on this man. He wasn't like other guys who she could best or control. Instinct told her that in a match of wills, the battle would be close and the victor not predictable.

"I'm good to go," Cecile said bravely.

And with that, Luke and Cecile headed down the aisle.

They didn't speak to each other again until after the ceremony, when he took her arm and they followed the newly married couple out. She lost him when she went to stand in the family receiving line, found him again during endless wedding party pictures that seemed to last ages. He disappeared when the photographer began the multigenerational family shots, which took forever since her entire family was there—her mother, father, Elizabeth and a bunch of aunts, uncles and cousins that Cecile saw only at events like these.

"Fun, isn't this?" her father asked during a father-daughter picture. Being in his late fifties, his hair had grayed substantially.

"Elizabeth's very happy. That's what matters," Cecile said.

"Just promise me you'll elope," her dad joked as the photographer gestured Elizabeth over for the next photo.

"No need to even mention me and marriage in the same sentence," Cecile said. "Lisa's engaged, though. You remember Lisa?"

"I do. Tell her to elope. Invest the money instead."

Cecile laughed, and as Elizabeth arrived to join them, everyone paid attention to the photographer's instructions. By the time the photos were finally finished, all Cecile wanted was a pair of comfortable tennis shoes. Barring that, she wanted a very large glass of white wine.

The limos were waiting for the last of the immediate family; the other guests and wedding party members were already enjoying an open bar and appetizers at the Millennium Knickerbocker's Crystal Ballroom while they waited for the bride and groom to arrive.

"You look like you could use this," a deep voice said when Cecile finally walked into the reception. "The line's terrible."

"Thanks." Cecile turned and gained a sudden new appreciation for Luke Shaw as she took the wineglass he offered. The line for the bar was eight deep.

"Just stick with me," Luke said. "I know my way around these things."

"I can tell," Cecile murmured appreciatively as she

rolled the wine over her tongue. "So are you giving a toast?" she asked.

"That's Devon's brother's job, and I'm glad of it," Luke admitted cheekily. "Can't stand the things. 'To the bride and groom. May your love last a lifetime and all that happy jazz.'"

Cecile arched her eyebrow. Here was a man she could identify with, especially if this was his attitude. "You sound cynical."

"Realistic?" Luke queried. "Don't weddings make all the single people feel like they're left out of some exclusive club?"

"Yes, they do, and you're a brave man to admit it," Cecile said.

That fabulous grin widened, revealing naturally pearly whites.

"I'll take that as a compliment," Luke said. "Of course, now I'm going to have to think of one for you. Can't be something cheesy or trite, though, or given right at this moment. Better when you don't expect it, that way you'll get the full effect."

Down, girl, Cecile told herself at his innuendo. She reminded herself that she'd earlier resolved not to get swept up in the wedding magic. And Luke was obviously a flirt. Cecile hadn't had a chance to question her sister further about the man, but any female with half a brain could gauge Luke Shaw's type.

Even Cecile couldn't say she was unaffected. He was like a tickle—welcome and yet needing to be stopped at the same time. He was sexy, and already other unattached women were giving him the eye. In fact, one of them was making her way over now. Cecile plastered on a smile as the daughter of one of her father's business associates came over. Cecile hadn't seen her since high school, but one thing could be said about Loretta— years later, the blonde was still stunning.

"Cecile," Loretta said in greeting. "I don't believe I've seen you in ages. You look terrific." She turned to Luke. "Hi, I'm Loretta Foster."

"Luke Shaw," he said easily as he shook her hand. Cecile noticed that Loretta's ring finger was bare, and that jogged a memory—Cecile's parents had told her last Christmas about Loretta's wedding and the subsequent scandal when her husband had had an affair with his secretary only a few months later.

"It's nice to meet you, Luke," Loretta said, her attention fully on him.

Cecile's negative reaction to Loretta's interest in Luke startled her. Surely Cecile couldn't be jealous. She hardly knew Luke. She might think he was sexy, but she wasn't going to pursue him. Or would she say yes if he asked her out? With her new career needing her full focus, she'd been thinking only of the wedding reception when talking earlier with Lisa, but suddenly the idea of a date with Luke held appeal. And so did not letting anyone else have him.

Cecile glanced at her wineglass. Time for a refill and some much-needed space so that she could figure out exactly why she suddenly felt muddled and as if she were walking on quicksand. Cecile focused. Loretta must have told Luke she was divorced, for she was saying, "Sometimes it just takes a person twice to get it right. Wouldn't you agree?"

"I wouldn't know," Luke said easily, his tone light. Cecile avoided meeting his glance and made the mistake of looking at Loretta.

"You've never been married?" Loretta asked. She appraised Luke like a rare commodity, and Cecile's hackles rose. "Your father's the real-estate developer?"

"Right on both counts," Luke said.

Loretta leaned closer. "And you've escaped the noose this long?"

Luke shrugged. "I was holding out for Angelina Jolie, but Brad Pitt stole her."

"Oh, aren't you funny," Loretta said, her smile wide. "I just love a sense of humor. It's so rare to find that in a man these days. Most of them are simply too serious. Old before their time."

Deciding not to be a third wheel and determined to maintain self-control, Cecile began easing her way toward the bar. Perhaps in her grape bridesmaid garb she could cut the line. There had to be some privileges for wearing a hideous dress.

"So are you here with a date?" Loretta asked Luke, expertly sliding her question into the conversation. Loretta was good, very good, Cecile thought as she somehow resisted the urge to roll her eyes heavenward. She took another step, but a firm grip grasped her left wrist and she found herself jerked backward.

And directly up against Luke Shaw. He fitted her

neatly into the curve of his right side, and somehow Cecile managed not to drop the wineglass she still held as her body responded to his on a primitive level.

"Actually, I am taken," Luke told Loretta before Cecile could utter one word of indignant protest about his actions. Blatant chemistry was making her want to do things with him she'd decided not to do. Then she made the mistake of looking at him.

Those blue eyes caught Cecile's, and she froze under his gaze's intensity and seriousness. "You see," Luke told Loretta with firm conviction, "Cecile's my date."

Chapter Three

She was his date? Since when?

Luke had totally misread her conversation with Lisa. But since Loretta was staring at her oddly, Cecile closed her mouth and played along. "I'm his date," she confirmed. The idea actually held appeal—he had her pinned against him, creating strange warmth that simply demanded exploring. The man was temptation.

"Isn't that sweet," Loretta said, her recovery upon processing the announcement flawless. "You make such a lovely couple. Oh, they're seating for dinner. We'll catch up a little later. I do want to hear more, like how you met."

"That sounds great," Cecile lied, knowing Loretta would disappear for good now that her prospect was gone. Cecile detached herself from Luke's grasp and waved the wineglass at him as Loretta disappeared from view. "I'm your date?"

"You have objections? I thought that served both of our purposes quite well. Still do. How can you hit on me if we're not together?"

Indignation roared. "Despite what you may have overheard me say on the phone, I also said I wasn't going to hit on you. You are impossible."

"I try," Luke said. "Especially if I get what I want."

"Lisa was teasing. And I said maybe I would pursue you, maybe I wouldn't." Cecile's heart raced. He wanted her?

"I like the 'maybe I would' part better," Luke said, totally unfazed. He reached forward and took the glass from her hand before she sprinkled the wine remnants everywhere. "Let me get you a refill and I'll meet you at the head table. Since we're seated next to each other, we can talk, if you're still so hot and bothered— although, trust me, I have a solution for that."

"I'm not hot and bothered," Cecile lied, but Luke simply strode off knowing the truth.

Her body craved his. Her mind liked his and he met her challenge for challenge. The chemistry flared almost out of control in all areas, especially the ones that mattered. She would be sitting next to the most infuriating man in the room. And the most attractive. Cecile made her way to her assigned spot. The bride and groom were already seated, and all around the room the guests were settling down at their tables.

Once the minister finished the blessing, a movement to her left indicated Luke had arrived. He set down her wine. "Thanks," Cecile said.

"You're welcome," Luke replied. "I'm totally at your service. Anything you need."

More loaded words, Cecile thought as a shiver of anticipation ran down her spine. Luke Shaw was not the type of man you could use up and then spit out. He was the type a girl should savor, like fine wine. Despite her earlier resolution, she was tempted to indulge…if only a little. Luke was like no man she'd ever met before. The pendulum was swinging toward "maybe I should."

"What are you thinking?" Luke whispered.

She twitched slightly, his breath causing her skin to warm. "I was thinking of grabbing one of those rolls," she said, lying again.

"Master of the art of changing the conversation," Luke declared.

"Absolutely," Cecile said. "I'm like a cat. I always land on my feet."

"Do you purr like a cat, too?" he asked, his tone smooth. "Would you like me to scratch you behind your ears?"

Thankfully she didn't have to reply to his question as the main course arrived. She quickly discovered she was too wired to eat the combination chicken-and-steak entrée. She picked at the delicious-looking salad and passed on the rolls.

Maybe the wine was going to her head. Her face did feel a little tingly, as if she'd used a good astringent. She picked up her fork and forced herself to eat the chicken so that something besides alcohol was in her stomach. Still, she didn't say no when the roving waiter came by and refilled her wineglass. She wasn't driving but instead taking a cab out to her parents' house in the suburbs.

"So are you going to dance with me?" Luke asked when Elizabeth and Devon went to cut the cake.

"I think we're scheduled to share one dance," Cecile said. The bride and groom's first number was a waltz, but she wasn't sure about the music for the wedding party dance that followed.

"I meant after that," Luke said, suddenly serious. "Despite my earlier corny lines, I'd like to get to know you."

"Let's see how the first one goes," Cecile said, his seriousness shaking her slightly. Just when she thought she had Luke pegged, he changed the rules. "I've always said you can judge a man by how he moves," she admitted.

"You have?" Luke's expression was one of interest.

"Oh, you can absolutely tell," Cecile said with a nod. "My sorority sisters and I used to bet on it. Like if a man dances like a constipated hamster. Or does the sprinkler."

"The sprinkler?"

"Yeah, when you put one hand behind your head like this—" Cecile put her left hand behind her head so that her elbow pointed outward "—then your right arm extends straight out and sweeps back and forth like one of those pulsating water jets." Cecile demonstrated.

Luke winced. "Yeah, I admit, that's pretty bad. Very common. And bad. Not one of my gender's finer examples."

Cecile drew her breath sharply through her teeth. "Exactly. Avoid at all costs."

"So if he's horrid on the dance floor, does that mean he's terrible in other endeavors, as well?"

"Eight times out of ten," Cecile admitted. Her face

reddened and she took a long sip of wine and stole a glance at him over the rim.

Luke appeared suitably horrified. Then he winked. "Lucky for you, I don't dance like that."

"We'll see," Cecile commented, the rush of adrenaline sending a jolt through her. She sipped her wine and stared at the empty glass. How had that happened so fast? Time to switch to water. If not, she'd probably do something she'd regret. Like jump Luke Shaw and find out what kind of moves he had, starting with planting her lips on his. She had no doubt he could kiss, and new leaf be darned. She understood now why men rammed their ships on the rocks when exposed to the sirens.

Kissing Luke was a delectable-sounding idea but, unfortunately, probably not a very wise one.

Then again, Cecile wasn't known for wise decisions when it came to men. Unlike Lisa, Cecile was impulsive. Mr. Right always turned into Mr. Wrong. It was a fact of her life. Cecile rose to her feet, her mind waffling. "If you'll excuse me for a moment…" she said.

Luke stood also, a chivalrous gesture indicating good breeding and refined manner. He had to stop impressing her! Requiring space, Cecile headed for the sanctity of the ladies' room. Getting her bearings and wits together was probably a smart idea. The man had crawled under her skin, made her want things she'd best avoid. He made her want to throw caution to the wind. He invited her to play with danger.

All night he'd had the upper hand, probably from overhearing her conversation. But Cecile wasn't one who left the status quo alone, especially when it wasn't tilted in her favor. She was almost thirty and ready to get serious about having it all. She was tired of simply attending weddings—darn it, she wanted her own.

She wanted marriage and a husband and a career. She had no idea what Luke's intentions were beyond the obvious that involved getting her horizontal.

But she could say no, no matter how tempted she was. Right?

LUKE WATCHED AS Cecile made her way toward the ballroom exit. Ladies' room, he surmised. She wove her way through the room, her posture tall and strong despite having had a lot of wine in a short period of time.

Her body had a natural sway to it, one that enticed despite being clad in purple fabric that did little to enhance. Luke had made a career out of studying people and he liked the lines of Cecile's neck. He liked the way her mouth moved and the way she raised both eyebrows when she gave him her dubious look.

He hadn't met a woman who'd interested him this much in a long, long time, which made toying with her fun. He'd pushed to see exactly how much she'd dish back. She'd met his challenges directly, which had impressed the heck out of him.

As for naming her his date, that pronouncement had taken even him by surprise, but once he'd voiced the words, he'd immediately been glad he'd said it. His better ideas often arrived spur-of-the-moment.

The idea of spending time with Cecile appealed. She

reminded him of one of those traditional Greek statues. She had classic features that didn't come from plastic surgery or perfectly applied makeup. He could sense a realism to Cecile that mirrored his own. He guessed that she lived with both feet planted fully in the moment, just as he did.

Bottom line, she was a person he wanted to get to know. In more ways than one.

But as Luke was thirty-five, he was beyond the one-night-stand mentality of his younger days. Sure, having sex was pleasurable, but the older he got, the more he realized quality was more important than quantity. He wanted to savor, to appreciate the woman. To enjoy her company for as long as it was mutually agreeable.

Luke hadn't met a woman like Cecile Duletsky in forever. Thankfully he was still seated, for parts of him had stirred to attention. Luke reached for his water goblet. He drained the contents in one long swallow, but that did little to quench the thirst he'd developed.

At this point in his life, he'd reached the place where he wanted it all, starting with finding the right woman who could hold her own. After all, he had everything else: condo, car, sailboat and a fantastic job. Those were all material possessions, just "stuff." In reality, nice but meaningless. What he needed was to find his other half. The way Devon had.

Luke wanted nothing less. That's why he tossed himself out there, dating now and then, trying to find his soul mate. As for Cecile, the gods had blessed him when they'd paired her with him tonight. Luke was a believer in fate, but he knew that to get a door to open you at least had to jiggle the handle. That's what he'd been doing with Cecile. Testing her.

She'd passed.

The bride and groom chose that moment to wander back to the head table and sip champagne from the engraved hand-blown flutes custom-made for the occasion. Strange to think that the neighbor Luke had grown up throwing mud and snowballs at had become Dr. Devon Pinewood, esteemed surgeon and happily married man.

Luke and Devon were about a year apart in age and had been a grade level apart at the private prep school they'd both attended. That hadn't stopped them from getting into loads of boyhood trouble over the years, even if lately the only trouble had been on the golf course when each tried to finagle his way to the lower score. Elizabeth had been a calming influence on Devon from the moment they'd met at a charity event four years ago. Luke smiled as he watched the couple. They'd had some rough spots but worked through them.

Hopefully Luke could also find that magic. Of course, he and Devon had different ideas of what comprised the perfect woman. Unlike Devon, Luke wanted his woman to be an independent spirit who vocalized her thoughts and stirred him up.

Cecile certainly got him going. Perhaps her assertive nature came with the hair—those strawberry-blond strands just begged a man to touch that human fire. Her hair fit her flamboyant and outgoing nature.

Devon's mother approached the head table. Mistress of the clock, she pointed to her watch. "It's time for the wedding party dances," she said. She scanned the room, mentally locating each member of the wedding party. "Where's Cecile?" she asked, directing the question at Luke.

"She's in the ladies' room," Luke said as he rose to his feet. "I'll go get her."

"Thank you." An expression of relief crossed Amanda's face, and Luke understood why Elizabeth's parents had simply ceded much of the control for the wedding. Luke didn't know much about the Duletskys, but a glance over at their table showed that they were having a relaxed and fun time.

Wise people, Luke noted.

He kept an eye out for Cecile as he left the ballroom, but he didn't see her. He exited, strolling toward the restrooms. He caught up with her just as she was leaving. She wasn't paying much attention and practically bumped into him.

"Steady," he said as he gripped her arms lightly to stop her from teetering. The dyed-to-match heels she wore weren't too stable.

Her green eyes widened as she recognized her savior. "What are you doing, following me around?" she demanded.

Yep, she was definitely the type who rallied. No one would ever mistake her for being passive, and Cecile was certainly unlike the women who subtly pointed out their availability as Loretta had done earlier. He and

Cecile were turning out to be very compatible, and he was finding her a perfect match for every one of his predetermined criteria. He liked the way she felt pressed against him. He enjoyed her wit and refusal to back away from a challenge. Her green eyes were hypnotic orbs he could drown in. Cecile was the entire package—beauty and brains. And she connected with him on all levels. If tonight went well, he was ready for it to be the first of many.

"Actually, yes, I was following you," Luke admitted. He slid his hands down her arms and curled her fingers into his palms. "It's time for me to show you my moves. We're wanted on the dance floor."

Chapter Four

She almost tripped again, but his hands continued to steady her. His touch created an odd tingling, something she'd been in the bathroom trying to avoid.

There was definitely a large amount of chemistry zinging between them, and for some reason Cecile was scared. Something about Luke made her feel as if she were in a fun house, on one of those moving floors that tilted you off balance.

"Elizabeth and Devon are sharing the first dance," Luke said as he led her back into the ballroom, his hand on the small of her back to guide her. "We're up next."

The lights had dimmed and a spotlight was trained on the center of the dance floor where Devon and Elizabeth were wrapped in each other's arms.

"Ready?" Luke asked.

Cecile trembled slightly. His touch had made her edgy, as if she were about to fall down a slippery slope—and yet something told her she'd love every minute of the dangerous experience. "You know, the wedding party having to dance is a silly ritual," Cecile said.

"You're such a romantic," Luke said, chuckling at her cynical attempt to disengage. "And I would normally agree with you, except that this ritual gets you into my arms, and for that I'm grateful. I'm looking forward to holding you."

That statement simply had Cecile closing her mouth, her glib reply dying on her lips. As much as the prospect of being close to him both appealed and frightened, she found herself wanting him to hold her. She'd had such a bad run with men, but she sensed that Luke was somehow innately different. Yet, was this just here and now? Or maybe something more?

"Let's go see how I dance," Luke said, not giving her a chance to contemplate her thoughts further. The confident gleam in his blue eyes spoke volumes.

The spotlight dance concluded, and within seconds she was out on the dance floor and pressed up against him. He slid his arm around her, his right hand splayed against the curve of her lower back. His moves were easy as they stepped in rhythm, a unity to their flow.

Heat began to rise, creating a flush that spread across Cecile's face and chest. If she wanted, she could easily lean her head forward and rest it on his shoulder, but instead she glanced over that shoulder and tried to stare into the darkness and decipher the mess her feelings had become.

She was older now, and this wedding had proved to her that she did want it all. Luke was the whole package. His fingers pressed against her, drawing her closer, his intentions clear. He was temptation personified, his moves a prelude to the night to come, should she choose to accept. The music ended.

"How'd I do?" he said, his deep voice holding a slightly husky quality.

"Too well," Cecile admitted and she detached herself and made her way over to the bar. Getting a drink would put some space between them. Never had a dance made her so rattled. She needed something to cool her off, maybe provide her some focus or at least rationale for this insanity. She ordered a glass of wine and a glass of water from the bartender and took both over to the table where her parents sat. An empty seat had opened up now that the dancing had started, and a waiter stopped by with wedding cake. He put several slices down. Seeing the bouquet toss was next, Cecile excused herself to wash her hands, deliberately missing the event. Knowing Elizabeth, she'd probably aim it directly at her, and while Cecile did want to find Mr. Right, she didn't need Luke getting any wrong ideas for she was sure he'd get the garter. Upon her return, she ignored the garter toss, ate some cake and made small talk with her parents.

About ten minutes later, black fabric entered into view on her left, and Cecile glanced up from finishing the last bite of her second piece. Luke.

"Did you save me any?" he asked, gesturing to the empty plates.

"No," Cecile said unapologetically. She glanced at her parents, but as if on cue, the music had changed to Glenn Miller's "In the Mood" and they were rising to their feet and heading hand in hand toward the dance floor.

"You know, you are a surprise," Luke said as he lowered himself into the chair next to her. "I thought you would have been out there with the bachelorettes."

"I didn't want to risk it," Cecile said. "Knowing my sister, she'd probably run over and hand me her throw-away bouquet."

Luke reached into his pocket and fished out a blue garter. He twirled it around his finger. "Like Devon did to me?"

"Exactly," Cecile said. She'd been right, which was why she'd deliberately put her back to the dance floor so she didn't have to watch the garter toss. She frowned.

As if sensing her question, Luke said, "I got out of having to dance with the girl who caught the bouquet. She was five."

"Oh," Cecile said.

Luke leaned over. "Jealous?"

"Ha," Cecile said, covering her fib with sarcasm.

"Then what would you call it?" Luke asked, not letting her off the hook.

"A simple case of avoidance?" Cecile suggested.

He shook his head, those surfer-blond locks glistening. "Nah, that's not what it is. You're not the type who avoids confrontation. If you didn't want a man's attention, you'd tell him to take a hike. I think you've just discovered that I'm more man than you can handle."

"In your dreams," Cecile said. She pushed the empty plate away. "Don't flatter yourself. I haven't seen my parents in a while, so I was spending time with them. I've been in New York up until this past week."

Luke simply arched an eyebrow. "So you've moved back home?"

"Not exactly. Back to my hometown. I grew up here, but I've been away since graduating high school. I just got a new job and so here I am."

"Here you are," Luke parroted.

"Right," Cecile said, at that moment deciding it was time for him to talk about himself. "What about you? Have you always lived here?"

"Pretty much," Luke said. "I went to Northwestern and have worked in Chicago ever since. So confirm something that's impressed me so far about you—you aren't the type of woman who plays typical games, are you?"

She tilted her head and studied him, trying to decide how best to answer. "You seem to think you know a lot about me."

"I don't. I'm pretty certain I have you typecast, though, but you do keep surprising me. I definitely would like to get to know you better, maybe take this 'date' to another level."

"Hmm. I'm sure you would," Cecile said, her fingertips keeping rhythm with the music as she let his words wash over her. She'd already indulged in an extra slice of wedding cake. What would Luke be like if she let herself have even just a taste of what the wedding magic promised? Would she regret saying no until the end of her days if she let this one moment slide by? Answer not forthcoming, she glanced at her empty wrist and exhaled in frustration. Her watch was in her bag under her chair at the head table. "Do you know what time it is?"

"Actually, yes." Luke stretched out his arm so that the tuxedo sleeve rode up, revealing a toned forearm and a platinum watch. "It's ten-thirty."

"Wow. That late already." The event ended at midnight. She glanced around. Many guests had already left. Others were crowding the dance floor.

"I guess time flies when you're having fun," Luke said.

"I suppose so," Cecile said. She blinked, a bit fuzzy from too much wine and a lack of sleep from the past few weeks. No matter how tempting Luke was, her conscience told her to say no to spending the night with him. She assumed that was what he'd meant when he'd asked to take things to the next level.

Of course, that part of her in overdrive wanted nothing more than to say yes, but what if he was just another Mr. Right Now? As much as they were easier to deal with, she was tired of having flings and was ready for more. If she passed on tonight's offer, she'd at least prove to herself that she'd changed, grown past indulgences that had no basis in anything but momentary passion. She wanted to wait for Mr. Right. If that was Luke, he'd understand. "I'm not planning on staying too much longer," she told Luke.

"Then you have to dance with me at least one more time," Luke insisted. The music changed, this time to a contemporary number. He rose to his feet and pulled Cecile with him. "Come on."

His fingers on hers incited, and Cecile allowed herself to be swayed. "Okay. Just one song," she said, especially since the faster numbers didn't allow for any intimate contact. Touching Luke planted ideas in her head, made her want to pursue him. And admittedly Luke was one of those men who made dancing enjoyable. She'd always loved to dance, and with Luke, one song slipped into two and then three as the band played all her favorite songs in a row.

Despite having a good time, she begged off when a slow number began and made her way to the head table to retrieve her purse. She slid the beaded strap onto her shoulder and turned to him. "This has been great. Thanks. I'll see you."

"Sure," Luke said. The moment was awkward and she knew he was disappointed, but she was exhausted, tired from her relocation and all the wedding events of the past week.

Although it might not be what she wanted, sleep sounded exactly like what she needed, so she left Luke and went to find her sister. Elizabeth was out on the dance floor, leading a version of "The Electric Slide," a staple at every wedding.

"You aren't leaving?" Elizabeth asked as she stepped to the side, the line dance continuing without her.

"I'm going to call it a night," Cecile confirmed with a nod.

Elizabeth's eyes widened. "But you can't! Devon and I are closing the place down, and I've barely gotten to talk to you. And what about Luke? Loretta said you're here with him."

"He just said that to keep her from hitting on him," Cecile said. A glance around the ballroom showed that Luke was nowhere in sight.

"He's a great guy, Cecile," Elizabeth said. "You should get to know him."

"Perhaps in the near future," Cecile said. "Right now I'm just ready to head back out to the suburbs."

"You should have just stayed here for the night like Mom and Dad," Elizabeth insisted. "Stop by the front desk and see if there's a room. I don't like the idea of you in a cab this late at night."

"Really, it's no big deal." Cecile sighed as she saw her sister's face. "Okay, fine. I'll ask. I've got a bag checked anyway that I need to pick up."

She took the elevator to the lobby and, because she'd given her word, approached the front desk. A minute later, the clerk told her the hotel was full. "I can find you something at a nearby hotel," he offered.

"No, that's not necessary," Cecile said. She'd simply take a cab to her parents' as she'd planned all along.

"Cecile?"

She turned upon hearing the familiar voice. She swallowed. Luke had loosened his bow tie and it hung down, exposing his neck and collarbone. "Hey, Luke," she said. "I thought you'd gone."

"No, I'm on my way out now. No sense in staying if you were leaving." He came closer, and her breath lodged in her throat. Even in the bright lobby lights he looked great.

"I'm waiting for them to retrieve my garment bag," Cecile said, the moment stretching.

"Ah," he said, stopping only an arm's length away.

Cecile's knees weakened slightly as she realized how

powerless she really was to the attraction she felt when around him. She also saw the moment for what it was: fate sending her another chance to say yes. Cecile was a firm believer in fate's signs. In college, she'd been torn between two sororities, but a last-second experience at one of the parties had been the incentive she'd needed to pick the Roses. From that choice, she'd gained her best friends. And until recently, her job in New York had been perfect, but when she'd been passed over for a promotion, Cecile had taken that as a sign to try for something new. That decision had led her to *The Allegra Montana Show.*

Now fate was thrusting Luke Shaw in front of her once more, a sign that perhaps turning down his offer had been the wrong decision. Twenty years from now, would she regret passing by this chance? Or should she seize the moment and have a grand passion to remember when the nights grew long and cold and she was alone?

As the bellhop returned with her bag, Luke took the suitcase from her hand. "I've got it," she protested.

"I'll take it," he replied, and she decided to let him carry her bag at least to the hotel's taxi stand. "Do you have your valet ticket?"

"I'm taking a cab out to my parents'," she said.

He paused and turned. "This late?"

"Yes. My apartment isn't too far, but it won't be ready until tomorrow afternoon."

The pupils in Luke's blue eyes darkened. "So stay with me."

"You're joking," Cecile said, flustered and voicing

the first thing that popped into her head. Luke had to be a mind reader. And worse, her libido was now fully wide-awake. And willing. Chemistry and fate made for a deadly, irresistible combination.

"I'm not kidding," Luke said, his forceful tone sending anticipatory shivers down her spine. He led her to the revolving doors. "I'm just a few blocks away."

"You've been hitting on me all night," Cecile said, following him out onto the street as if he were the pied piper.

"Yes, I have," Luke told her. They'd stopped right outside the taxi stand. "I'm not an animal, Cecile. My parents raised a gentleman. I won't lie and tell you that I don't want you. I will tell you that I'll keep my hands off you if that's what you'd like. You need a place to stay and I have one. So what do you say? I'll drive you home tomorrow, when both of us are thinking more clearly. If not, I'll see you to your cab."

The doorman stood discreetly a few feet away. Luke nodded to him, and the man waded out into the street, blew his whistle and hailed a taxi. Luke handed the man her bag.

The cabbie started loading the suitcase into the trunk, then opened the passenger door and waited for her.

Luke reached out and put his hand on her arm. "It was great meeting you," he said.

No! Cecile inwardly shouted as her body overrode any misgivings her head might have. Fate had given her another chance, and she wasn't going to let this opportunity slip through her fingers.

And her only reason would be that she was trying to

be a good girl, holding out for a Mr. Right who might never come.

Scarlett O'Hara had it right. Tomorrow was another day.

"You are getting in with me, aren't you?" Cecile asked. Luke paused and tilted his head. She had him with her next words. "I don't think I know what directions to give him to your place."

It took less than five minutes to reach his high-rise building, less than a minute to take the elevator up sixty-eight floors. Anticipation hummed between them, and Cecile tried to concentrate on her surroundings. While the outside was simply a normal rectangular skyscraper with few architectural details, inside, Luke's living room soared a dramatic two stories. The space was light, bright and modern. Minimalist pieces and modern art dominated the space. The first floor consisted of the living room, a dining area, a kitchen to make any cook jealous, a full hall bath and the second bedroom. Upstairs contained Luke's loft office and, beyond that, the master bedroom suite. Her apartment was a shoebox compared to this.

"Can I get you something to drink?" he asked. "Wine? Beer? Soda?"

"Water?" Cecile suggested, suddenly extremely nervous and not wanting any more alcohol. Sure, she'd been in this type of situation before, but this time she was with Luke. And that made her nerves feel like egg-shells. While she wanted this man, she wanted whatever happened between them to be worth the buildup. She didn't want crass. Or tawdry. She stared out the floor-to-ceiling windows that afforded a phenomenal view of Lake Michigan and the well-lit Navy Pier.

"Here you go," Luke said a few moments later as he returned and handed her a glass of water. "Are you hungry? I can have some food delivered. Or I make a mean omelet."

"I'm fine," Cecile said. She noticed he'd stripped out of the tuxedo jacket and removed the bow tie.

She took a long drink, for her throat had gone dry. Luke was sexy. Very sexy. Too sexy for his own good. What was she doing here? He was like chocolate cake. Sinful. Decadent. Worth the guilt. She'd never been one to be able to resist what was forbidden, especially when fate intervened.

"Do you believe in wedding magic?" Cecile asked.

He frowned slightly. "Define what you mean."

She tapped the glass with her forefinger. "The feeling that there's something in the air at weddings. Something that makes people do things they shouldn't."

"I know what you're talking about," Luke said.

"So was that why you were hitting on me?"

Luke had chosen water, as well, and he sputtered slightly as a sip went astray. "No. I hit on you because you're a very beautiful, desirable woman. Surely you know that."

"You didn't just want to pick me up, have some fun, enjoy a quick roll in the hay?" she pressed.

"I'm not afraid of going home alone at the end of the night," Luke said. "I wasn't staking out the hotel lobby."

"No?" Cecile's body reacted to his honesty. She'd

come willingly to his house, but she'd had to question him to be positive she was about to make the right choice. For some reason, it was important she not be a notch on his belt, important that, had she turned him down, he wouldn't have just turned elsewhere.

"No," Luke said. "From the first moment I saw you I wasn't settling for anything less. Why else would I leave after you did?"

"I have to admit, you've been tempting me all night," she heard herself say. If he was turned on, so was she. Life had a way of putting her in situations like this, making her realize that leopards couldn't change their spots. And with a man like Luke Shaw, who wanted to change in the first place?

"So what are you going to do?" Luke asked, his voice silky and seductive.

"I haven't decided," Cecile said, although in reality she had. She needed release and fulfillment. She was a woman with needs, and hers hadn't been met in a while. She didn't want Bob. She desired flesh and blood. She wanted to be driven over the edge and into the abyss. She wanted Luke.

And with that, all her resolutions to say no flew out the window. She'd start over tomorrow.

"Is there anything I can do to help you decide?" Luke asked. He'd moved toward her, almost as close as he'd been during that first slow dance.

She'd been seduced before but never like this. Luke was out of her league. Her body already hummed, and she was damp. "You don't make anything easy, do you?" she asked, her voice hoarse.

"Never," Luke said. He reached out and ran a finger down her bare arm. She shivered but not from cold. "I get what I want, Cecile. Always have, always will."

"And what do you want?" Cecile said, her breath lodging in her throat as she waited for his reply.

"I want you," Luke said, his tone forceful and determined. A thrill shot though her. "And I definitely want this."

With that, he lowered his mouth and kissed her.

Chapter Five

The man could kiss. Oh, maybe it was because she couldn't remember the last time she'd been kissed like this, but Cecile didn't think so. Luke Shaw was simply the master. He pressed her shoulders up against the plate-glass window and plundered her mouth like an experienced sexual pirate.

She heard herself moan as he raked his teeth across her tongue, felt herself shake as his hands gripped her buttocks and drew her lower half forward so that her body molded to his.

He ran his tongue over her lips, teasing and cajoling. His lips lingered, pleasuring her with an endless kiss that robbed her senses. Time stopped as Cecile simply let herself enjoy. Then he slid his lips to the side, over her cheek and over to her right ear. "Follow me," he said.

At this moment she might let him lead her anywhere, but he led her upstairs into his bedroom. Here again he had floor-to-ceiling windows but this time with a western view. He left the lamps off, undressing her in the muted glow of the city lights coming through the sheers.

He unzipped the purple dress and let the offensive garment pool at her feet. Lowering his lips, he kissed his way over the skin he'd exposed. He suckled her through her bra, and when she cried out with pleasure, he unhooked the purple lace and tossed it away. Then he replaced his mouth and danced his tongue over her sensitive peaks.

"You are so beautiful," he told her. And unlike other men who'd said that line, with Luke she believed. He raised his hands to remove the pins in her hair and sent the updo tumbling down. The strands cascaded to the tops of her breasts, and he lifted a lock to his lips. "I love this color. So fiery and lovely against your skin."

And then he kissed her neck before he began to work his way lower. All Cecile could do was let the pleasure wash over her in waves. She reached for him, but Luke brushed her hands away. "Enjoy," he commanded, and as he stripped away her matching purple underwear and lowered himself to his knees, she simply obeyed his instructions as the bliss began.

She clutched the top of his head for support as pleasure rocked her, and then finally he was standing, kissing her mouth and carrying her to his bed. He threw the coverlet aside and placed her on the soft sheets. His fingers were everywhere, and Cecile groaned as he spread her legs and worked her into frenzy. Then he removed his own clothes, freeing a part of him that strained for attention. He was a big man and perfectly proportionate. He protected himself, leaned over her and slid inside.

"Oh," Cecile said as her body adjusted to his presence. He fit her well, and she quivered as the first of her releases began. He stroked easily, sending her into multiple valleys and crests, each one exponentially more pleasurable than the rest. He kissed her eyelids, kissed her lips, kissed her breasts. He slid in and out, his body matching her rhythm until he shattered them both in a climax unlike any Cecile had experienced.

She'd never been so satiated. She and Tori had often complained to each other that after lovemaking the woman was often still so wired that she felt like she could go outside and run a marathon. But not this time. Not with Luke.

The man could dance. He could make love. Both superbly. He drew her into his arms, and her body rested, spent and totally fulfilled.

"Good?" he asked.

"Phenomenal," she told him, and then her eyes began to close.

"I'm glad. I'll be back in a second. Just rest."

She heard him enter the bathroom, and within moments he'd returned and curled her to his side as if she had belonged there forever. She decided she liked it and, within moments, drifted away.

ONCE HE WAS SURE she was sleeping, Luke slipped from the bed to retrieve her suitcase. She'd want it in the morning.

When he returned, he set the case on the floor and took a moment to stand there in the muted light and study her. She was beautiful. There was no other word for it. Her strawberry-blond hair fell about her shoulders in waves, the style from the wedding long gone. He had kissed her creamy skin everywhere, and he let his gaze trace a path down her body to the small of her back. His sheets hid, yet outlined, the rest of her—those long legs that had wrapped around him tightly and taken him to heights never imagined.

His first impression of her had been right—she was everything he wanted in a woman. He'd dated enough to know the difference between lust and love. He knew the difference between "this is a woman I want to do" and "this is a woman I want to have."

Cecile fit in the latter category. He was a realist and perhaps a little jaded. She had asked him if he believed in wedding magic. Magic was Santa Claus or the Tooth Fairy. It had a time and a purpose. However, that didn't discount that something had happened between him and Cecile, something new and different, as if the right key had finally fit the lock of a place he subconsciously kept guarded.

There was a country song about a man seeing a woman and immediately imagining the dress and the church and happily ever after. Luke had no such immediate illusions with Cecile, but Luke knew that something was different this time, and it demanded further exploration. Luke slid into bed and curled her to him.

She sensed his presence for she rolled to face him.

"Hey," she said, immediately awake. She touched his chest, and Luke tried to fight the desire that overtook him as she moved her lips to his. Somehow he'd slow this relationship down. Tonight would not be a one-night stand. Not by a long shot.

WHEN SHE FIRST WOKE up that morning, Cecile needed several seconds to remember where she was. And exactly what she'd done. She leaned up on her elbow. The bedside clock read nine-fifteen. She lowered herself back down onto the pillow and stared at the ceiling for a moment. Beside her, Luke slept on, his breathing steady and regular.

Cecile's heart raced a little, and she worked to steady herself. How many times during the night had he reached for her? How many times had they made love? Each time he'd wanted her, she'd woken up and found herself ready and willing.

Her body ached from all the pleasures it had blissfully endured. Luke was a generous and giving lover, and she'd enjoyed every moment she'd spent with him. Her only regret? That it was time to let the magic end and get back to the real world. Sure, Luke had said last night that he'd drive her home, but Cecile was independent. As much as she'd like to stay here, mornings after were always awkward. She'd let him sleep and leave a goodbye note.

Besides, she'd made herself a vow. *Tomorrow* had arrived. Despite the connection she'd experienced, Cecile's cynicism had returned with the light of day. Good sex wasn't a foundation for a relationship.

Cecile slipped from the bed and slid into her under-garments only. Luke had retrieved her suitcase and she'd grab something out to wear for the ride home. She refused to travel to the suburbs in a bridesmaid's dress.

She frowned as she wadded up her clothes and made one more sweep of the room before padding her way down the stairs, now clad in black knit pants and a red short-sleeve sweater. She zipped the bridesmaid dress and heels inside the suitcase and glanced around. She had her purse. She wore the flip-flops she'd worn to the salon for her bridal party pedicure. She had just about everything. Opening her purse, she drew out her watch and slipped that on before reaching for her phone.

Her cell phone! That was still in Luke's tuxedo pocket! Cecile glanced around the living room. He'd taken the jacket off last night before they'd gone upstairs. Where had he put it? Kitchen? The morning sun was flooding through the huge eastern windows, the Sunday-morning lake view beautiful. She knew she didn't have much time before Luke stirred.

She found the jacket tossed onto the back of a dining room chair. Snagging her phone, she flipped it open. No messages. She tucked the device into her purse and surveyed the condo a final time. Time to leave a note. Leave her phone number.

She paused. That would defeat leaving things as they were. While she sensed Luke was somehow different, her jumping into his bed had proven that, while she'd had good intentions, she wasn't different. She hadn't resisted acting on her urges. She'd still chosen a Mr. Right Now instead of searching for Mr. Right.

No, maybe things would be better simply left in silence. He could always ask her sister if he really wanted to track her down. And it wasn't as if she didn't know where to find him should she change her mind.

Once out in the main room, Cecile made her way to the front door. She again glanced around one final time, her mind once more debating the subtleness of just running out. Then she stilled the indecision in her head, reached for the door handle and left.

LUKE HADN'T SLEPT so well, or so late in quite a long while. He stretched, his feet not quite reaching the end of his California king-size bed. He felt great. That was saying something, actually. Normally after a night of truly excellent sex he was a little wiped out. Content but not very rested. This time everything had been beyond perfect. Despite the lack of sleep, his body had never been so alive or so in tune. Making love to Cecile had been incredible, better than anything else he'd experienced.

He reached for her and discovered she wasn't there.

Luke frowned and sat up immediately. He hadn't closed the drapes, but it was clear it was still morning, and a glance at the clock told him it was almost ten. When had she left? And how had he not woken up? He'd always woken up before.

Then again, he'd never made love to Cecile before. Everything about her—and everything about last night—had been different.

Sure, at the start of the wedding reception they'd simply been toying with each other, seducing each other with words. Then she'd said yes, and when they'd arrived at his apartment, things had become turbo charged. For him, that first kiss had changed the stakes. He'd wanted her, and not just to slake some lust. Last night hadn't been about indulging in temporary wedding magic, as she'd called it. He'd experienced a connection, darn it. Hadn't she?

Maybe he didn't have her pegged as thoroughly as he thought he did. She'd surprised him yet again. He tossed off the sheet, pulled on some boxers and made his way downstairs. The part of him expecting a note quickly found itself disappointed. She'd vanished without a trace, forgoing a goodbye.

Although, he knew how to find her. But that raised another question. Should he even try? Cecile was a beautiful and frustrating woman, a perfect oxymoron of tempting flesh. He checked his tuxedo pocket and, disappointed, shook his head. She was thorough; she'd even remembered her phone. He entered the kitchen and started his coffeemaker. He could decide what to do about her later. That he wasn't ready to let her vanish so easily was a given. But first he had work to do. He'd brought it home on Friday when he'd cut out early so that he could be on time for the wedding rehearsal.

As senior producer for *The Allegra Montana Show,* it was his job to oversee the entire production from start to finish. While each segment had its own producer, they all reported to Luke.

He was the show runner, the one who oversaw every episode and made sure they all fit Allegra's format. He reported directly to Allegra herself. Although Luke had known her both professionally and socially for years, this was the first time he'd ever worked for her. So far, the transition from her former show runner to Luke had gone smoothly.

Luke enjoyed working for Allegra, and that he'd been hired had meant he didn't have to leave Chicago to seek high-quality employment, making the situation win-win. Long ago Luke had vowed to work in television but preferably not in either New York City or Los Angeles. He'd gotten his degree from Northwestern University's Medill School of Journalism and after that had gone on to find employment locally, doing stints and producing shows for the local FOX and PBS affiliates until he'd worked his way up to the title of assistant producer of *The John Ryan Show.*

When Ryan had retired, Luke had found himself out of a job. On advice of Luke's father, who'd brokered the commercial real estate end of the deal, Allegra had moved into both Ryan's open time slot and his expansive studios, which she'd quickly remodeled to make her own. Despite Luke's talent and connections, he hadn't been a shoo-in for a place on her staff. When her show runner quit to move to New York, logic said she'd hire internally, and Luke had had to campaign hard and call in some favors to convince her he was a better choice. Finally she'd said yes, and Luke had literally moved back into his old office.

The workweek was intense, but Luke wouldn't change what he did. Monday and Tuesday were preproduction, the rest of the week taping and postproduction. He oversaw tons of meetings, approved the scripts and the talent. He reviewed the research, discussed upcoming ideas and coordinated the budget. He oversaw the taping of six shows: five of those edited and shown the next week, one shown the following. Allegra, the first Hispanic talk-show host to reach Oprah-like numbers, took her commitment to her show very seriously. She taped almost year-round with very few weeks off.

His coffee finished dripping, Luke poured himself a cup and took the black brew upstairs to his office. He settled himself into his leather desk chair and looked wistfully out at the lake. He'd much rather be sailing, but he wanted to go into tomorrow's meeting with a clear plan of exactly how to acclimate the new assistant producer into her role. He didn't want to toss the person in feetfirst and tell her to swim.

While she had delegated other responsibilities to him, Allegra still hired her production staff herself and she'd forwarded the folder on the new employee Friday morning. She'd declared the candidate from New York better than good, and Luke trusted his boss. Allegra was always on top of everything, but since the new AP had requested some time between her hiring date and starting date, the personnel folder hadn't been a high priority until late last week.

Luke opened his briefcase, took out the interoffice envelope and uncurled the string that held the flap closed. Whoever had been hired better be a fast learner and quick on her feet. That was all he asked. The ease of his job depended on how well she could do hers.

He slid the file folder out of the envelope and flipped it open. Immediately he did a double take as he read Cecile Duletsky's name.

Luke's jaw set into a tight line. He read over her résumé and job portfolio. Boy, had he messed up this situation. No wonder she'd fled. Had she known who he was? Perhaps he should have asked those mundane questions, such as, "What do you do?" before bedding her.

Those details had seemed so irrelevant at the time.

He figured they'd have this morning to make small talk, but she'd left. He wanted to throttle her and kick himself in the rear a few hundred times, as well. Wasn't this just a wicked twist of fate? The more he thought about it, he doubted she had any idea he was her new boss. If she'd meant to seek him out, the night would have gone down differently, with Cecile being more aggressive.

The end result, however, was that Luke's life was about to become extremely interesting, if not downright difficult.

He studied Cecile's file again. She fit his description of an ideal hire: she was fast on her feet and a self-starter. She'd produced several shows he'd seen, and knowing that was *her* work impressed him. She was extremely qualified.

In all areas.

He sipped his coffee as once again his anger grew. Such a perfect night wasted. He'd wanted to get to know her. Last night he'd just begun to scratch the surface. He'd had such hopes that this time he might have found someone suited to him, someone worth investing some deep emotional energy.

Fat chance of that now. She'd asked if he believed in wedding magic. Everyone knew magic didn't last.

He took a moment and tried to picture the shock on Cecile's face when she discovered he was her boss. She said she always landed on her feet. That was going to be interesting to see. For if Cecile thought she was going to get the upper hand on him at work, she was in for one rude awakening.

Chapter Six

"So how was the wedding?" Allegra asked. She sat behind a huge mahogany desk and barely glanced up as Luke entered. He took a seat and waited while she finished reading the script. Closing it, she removed the reading glasses that no one outside of her production staff saw her wear. Her brown eyes focused on him.

Luke folded his hands into his lap. "The wedding went great. It was too bad my parents had to miss it, but their cruise couldn't be rescheduled."

"So there were no glitches?" Allegra asked. "No need to have them on the show, like that poor couple who had everything that could have gone wrong go wrong?" She finally cracked a slight smile. Luke knew she was still trying to figure out why he'd requested this meeting. She was one of the sharpest fifty-six-year-olds he knew, not that she looked fifty-six. Allegra wore blue today and she'd put her long dark hair up in a chignon that reminded Luke of Cecile's updo at the wedding.

"There was one tiny glitch," Luke admitted.

Allegra waited, a technique she used with her interview subjects, who felt inclined to fill the silence.

"Cecile Duletsky," Luke began. He'd debated telling Allegra for almost the whole of yesterday but had come to the conclusion that honesty was the best policy, especially here. Offense being the best defense and so forth. Luke knew Allegra. She was the type who liked all the cards out on the table. She was a straight shooter. If she found out about Luke and Cecile later, she'd feel ambushed, angry. That still didn't mean Luke liked admitting anything.

"Our new AP?" Allegra prodded.

"Yes."

"What about her?" Allegra said. "I'm meeting with her in a half hour. Since she was in New York and I'd already interviewed her once face-to-face for your position, this time I did her interview over the phone."

"She's the sister of Devon's wife, Elizabeth. She was a bridesmaid."

Allegra waited, but when Luke remained quiet she simply said, "Oh."

"Oh," Luke said, knowing Allegra understood what he was saying without voicing the words.

"You know how I feel about interoffice fraternization," Allegra said, crossing her arms and gazing at him, her head tilted slightly as her mind processed the ramifications of the situation.

"That's why I'm letting you know now. I don't want gossip reaching your ears, which is why I'm here. If anyone is to be held responsible, I want it to be me. I pursued her this weekend, not knowing she was the new AP until I read her file yesterday."

"Hmm," Allegra said. She reached forward and held a pen between two fingers. She tapped it idly on the desk, the staccato sound filling the silence. "I dislike awkwardness anywhere in my studio," she said finally. "I take it she has no idea who you are."

"She doesn't, and there won't be any awkwardness," Luke promised. Cecile had run out, after all, and hadn't found an excuse to contact him since then. "She's a true professional. I'm sure she'll want this kept quiet as much as I do."

"Yet you still like her?"

"Yes," Luke admitted. "But I'll handle it appropriately. Nothing will interfere with the running of this show."

"I'm going to hold you to that," Allegra said. Her brown eyes narrowed slightly. "Despite our friendship over the years, business is business. Luke, if you screw this up and bring drama to my studio, the first person I will fire is you."

"I understand," Luke said. He'd expected nothing less. He rose to his feet.

"Then we're clear," she said.

"Absolutely." Luke glanced at his watch. "I have a meeting with Susan in five minutes."

"Then I'll see you later," Allegra said. "Don't forget what I said."

"I won't." And with that Luke left Allegra's office, her words ringing in his ear.

THE PRODUCTION offices of *The Allegra Montana Show* consisted of several floors that had been added on in the early nineties to an old theater, which served as the studio. Allegra had wanted her producers to have ambient space in which to work. She'd created large offices along the outside walls, each with its own windows and outside view since Allegra felt that sunlight inspired creativity. The offices didn't have four solid walls dividing them from the interior but instead were glass rooms that had vertical blinds that closed to allow for privacy.

Cecile hadn't seen these facilities during either interview and she took everything in as she followed her assistant Janice to the eight-by-ten room that would be her office. Cecile had a western view of Highway 94 off in the distance, and this time of day traffic crawled.

She'd been in meetings all morning, and this was her first time stepping foot into her space. Desk. Leather chair. Computer table with desktop unit and portable laptop. Bookcases. File cabinets. Two guest chairs. Just about everything she'd need aside from some homey, personalized touches. The blinds were open, revealing a view of the noisy copy machines and, next to that small alcove, the elevators. Yep, she was definitely last man in.

"So are you excited?" Janice asked.

"I'm ready for this challenge. It should be fun." Cecile saw the younger girl's doubtful expression and smiled. "Well, hard work but fun. I'm a workaholic and this is what I like to do. I've been on vacation for the past few weeks—I had my sister's wedding and my move from New York—so I'm eager to get back to work."

"I'm looking forward to working with you," Janice said. Cecile figured the young girl had to be about her sister's age. "I heard that you produced that report on the hidden costs of drug abuse. That was some fantastic television."

"Thanks," Cecile said. She glanced at her watch. Just a little after one. She'd just finished lunch, basically a quick sandwich from the deli around the corner. "What time did you say my next meeting was?"

"The producers' meeting is two. On the agenda is this week's filming schedule and brainstorming the ideas for two weeks from now. All the stuff for this week's tapings was wrapped up this morning."

Janice pointed to the computer. "You're already set up on e-mail, and I've left a phone extension list on your desk—or you can always use the company directory button. Also, that folder contains the scripts for the shows taping this week. You're to read them so that you can get a feel for what's been dubbed the 'Allegra concept.'"

"I heard about that in more depth when I met briefly with Allegra this morning. She told me she's moving her image to the next level, but she still wants to be able to relate to her viewers and be seen as accessible and trustworthy."

"Allegra wants to be taken seriously," Janice said. "She's someone who truly cares. I've been here two years and there've been a lot of changes already, all exceedingly positive. And I do have to say, overall this is a great place to work."

"Excellent. That's why I signed on. Okay, I'd better read this stuff. Again, thanks for the welcome and agreeing to show me the ropes."

"No—thank you. I can already tell that you're going to be a lot better than the gal who had this office before. She was a diva." Janice covered her mouth with her hand. "Oops."

"Don't worry. I won't tell," Cecile said. She liked Janice. "How about we meet before the end of the day to touch base? Make sure I didn't miss anything important?"

"That'll work," Janice said. She exited the room and paused at the door. "Open or closed?"

Cecile had worked in worse office environments, and the copying noise really wasn't that distracting. Wanting to fit in, she asked, "What's the unwritten rule?"

"Open at all times unless you need to keep things private or don't want to be disturbed. Then, door closed. Really private, close the blinds."

"Got it. Leave the door open." And with that, Cecile turned her attention to the folder her boss had left for her. A note that read "Welcome aboard. See you at two," had been paper-clipped to the top.

That's nice, Cecile thought. She'd wanted to pick Janice's brain a little more about her boss but hadn't wanted to seem too curious. She'd find out everything she needed to know in less than an hour. Cecile opened the folder and began to read. The last thing she wanted was to be ill-prepared. As it was, her first night in her new apartment had been restless. She hadn't realized how much Luke had affected her. She refocused. First impressions were everything, and she planned to make a good one.

ONE-FIFTY. THE SECOND hand moved slowly around the decorative clock with an annoying *click, click, click*. Luke tapped his pencil. He couldn't believe he was nervous. He shouldn't have any jitters.

He'd known what Allegra was going to say. The irony was that he could do an entire show on his current misfortunes. "I met the woman of my dreams and I'll be fired if I touch her."

But I still want to risk it.

He sighed. Wedding magic was a potent and nasty thing, he decided. Since Devon and Elizabeth had put off their three-week honeymoon until the end of the month, Luke had met them for dinner in their new house last night, and gotten the scoop on Elizabeth's sister.

Cecile, Luke had learned, was the free spirit in the family. She went solo to events that were couples-only. She dated, Elizabeth thought, but wasn't really into long-term relationships. She'd never brought any men home to meet the parents, instead saying that no one had intrigued her long enough to be "the one."

"She looks for Mr. Right, but they always end up being Mr. Wrong," Elizabeth had confided over a glass of red wine. "Cecile's not one to waste time."

She certainly hadn't wasted time leaving his place, and it grated that she'd tossed him aside so quickly.

Hadn't she felt anything? He'd been intrigued, willing and wanting more than a night. And now he would see her more—but not the way he wanted. He had to work with her. Pleasantly—or be fired from a job he really liked and had fought to get.

Since Luke prided himself on being a good boss, he'd put aside such petty inclinations of wanting to surprise her. But in five minutes he was about to do just that. He'd meant to have a private moment with her all day, but she'd had employment paperwork to fill out upon her arrival, a name-badge photo to take and several meetings.

His schedule had been just as busy. And so as much as Luke wanted to warn Cecile, he couldn't place a note in her folder, *Hi, great night. Sorry you ran out. Surprise, I'm your boss.* He'd instead written something generic.

He guessed he could have been chivalrous and called Cecile, but since she'd run out on him, he'd decided the course of least resistance was for him to pretend to be as surprised as she was going to be. Her previous bosses had said she was a quick thinker, so Luke figured she'd be back on top of things quickly. He tamped down the image of when she'd been on top of him. Work called.

He glanced at the clock and rose to his feet. Two minutes until the meeting started. His files were already in the conference room, freeing his hands. He'd stroll in unencumbered, a man in control. But she was a woman who made him lose control, and he needed to fight the desire to head to her office, shut the door and kiss her senseless. He swallowed. Time to find out exactly what Cecile was made of.

CECILE WALKED INTO the production meeting room at three minutes to two. She'd planned on being early, but already three other people were in the room, standing at the end of a modern conference table that could easily seat twelve. The two men and one woman swiveled their heads and stopped midconversation.

"Hi," Cecile said, aiming for a confident yet not cocky first impression. "I'm Cecile Duletsky."

"Hi, Cecile," the fifty-something woman said as she stepped forward and extended her hand to shake Cecile's. "It's nice to meet you. I'm Susan. This is Ricky, and this guy over here is Matt."

They greeted Cecile and shook her hand, and by that time two more people entered the room and introduced themselves. Cecile had studied the notes her boss had left in her office. Depending on the complexity and depth of what the shows required, each producer was responsible for one or more segments filmed per week.

Joining today's meeting were the two line producers, who were the people responsible for the show's overall budget, as well as the money spent per episode.

"Why don't you sit here next to me," Susan said.

"Thanks," Cecile said, withdrawing her chair. "Does Allegra come to these meetings often?"

"Sometimes," Susan said as she pulled out her own seat. "However, that spot doesn't always go empty. Sometimes someone from Postproduction, Research, Promotion or Talent might come in if needed. You'll meet a lot of those people before Friday, although since we're on a shortened schedule, Research won't pitch ideas again until next week."

"I thought we're in charge of brainstorming?"

"We are. We brainstorm ideas and give them to Research. They find out how viable they are and send them back. Right now we've got the current ideas narrowed, but we need to decide how we're going to film them and who's going to produce each segment."

"Oh," Cecile said. While each talk show or variety show worked under the same general operating principles, each one had a different approach. Cecile knew she'd get used to the routine here soon enough. She studied her coworkers. The only one missing was the show runner, and she felt a rush of air at her back as her boss brushed by her. He'd arrived.

"Hi, everyone," he said. When Cecile glanced down the table, his head was bent almost to his chest as he searched for something in the file folder he'd opened on the table. Something seemed oddly familiar about him, and Cecile wished she could see his face so she could place him. "Sorry I'm late. I had a last-minute phone call that I'll tell you about in a second."

Although she didn't yet have a good glimpse of his face, his blond hair and voice were sending a chill down her spine. Now that he'd spoken again, she'd realized she knew that voice—but, no, it couldn't be possible.

"Let's get started right away," he said. "Our new assistant producer has joined us for her first day. Welcome—" he tapped the file folder "—Cecile."

He glanced up then and looked directly at her. Cecile froze. The nightmare was real. Her boss was Luke Shaw.

And he was staring at her with a slightly shocked expression that to anyone else in the room would simply appear to be welcoming. Cecile's eyes narrowed slightly as she saw through his *surprised* ruse. He'd known exactly who she was long before she'd sat down. The question was, had he known at the wedding?

But Luke was already moving on, a model of professional decorum in his blue Dockers pants and a polo shirt.

"Cecile, would you take a few minutes and introduce yourself to everyone? They haven't had the good fortune of reading over your résumé like I have," Luke said.

Oh, the cad. Even if this was standard operating procedure, he was…he was infuriating. She remembered his handwritten note and fumed. *Welcome aboard. See you at two.* The jerk! He could have at least warned her.

But then again, she had run out on him yesterday morning. Payback. She recalled telling herself not to do anything stupid her first week back in Chicago. She'd tempted fate and lost. Little wonder why she never played cards.

Cecile rose to her feet, glad she'd worn black knit pants and a mint-green short-sleeve cotton sweater. The shade added color to her now pale face and gave her some much-needed confidence as Luke crossed his arms. He was waiting to see her stumble. She refused to give him that satisfaction. Luckily she was almost at the opposite end of the table.

"Hi, everyone, I'm Cecile Duletsky and the quick

version is that I graduated from the University of Missouri with a journalism degree and I picked up my masters from Columbia University in New York. While in New York I worked as a segment producer for CBS and MTV. I'm a native Chicagoan and a die-hard sports fan. Da Bulls, Da Bears and Da Cubs—that's me."

And with that, she thumped back down in her seat.

"Thank you," Luke said. He lifted some papers and began to distribute them. "Everyone turn to page three. We'll start there."

He still hadn't sat down, and as Susan gave Cecile a packet, she whispered, "Nice short greeting. That'll win you loads of brownie points with everyone. And don't stress. Luke never sits at the beginning of a meeting. He's got too much energy."

He did have too much energy. Cecile had witnessed that firsthand. He'd recovered from lovemaking much faster than other men. He'd been insatiable. He'd been passionate and giving. Currently he was being professional, at least giving her the courtesy of pretending she was just another new hire. She had no doubt he would wait until an appropriate time and rake her over the coals. Although, then again, maybe not.

As she observed the meeting and watched Luke in his element, Cecile realized she'd been wrong about him. The night of the wedding she'd only thought of him as Luke Shaw Jr., son of the real estate developer. She hadn't even bothered to ask his occupation, much less dig beneath his surface in a more relevant way….

Now, watching him in his element, Cecile wanted to

smack herself in the forehead for her stupidity. Wait until Lisa, Tori and Joann heard about this gaffe. Once she was alone in the privacy of her apartment, she was going to need to reach out and call someone for moral support.

But right now she needed to pay attention. Luke was whipping through the agenda. Cecile found herself saying little unless asked directly for her opinion. Mostly she paid attention and listened, absorbing details about her five coworkers' personalities. Kate and Donna, the two budget minders, often played devil's advocate. Susan was a practical thinker; Ricky and Matt often came up with wild, outside-of-the-box ideas that Kate and Donna poked holes in. The goal, of course, was to get ratings while still having a show with integrity.

"Okay, that about wraps it up," Luke said. He'd sat down in his chair at some point, the motion unnoticed in the whirlwind discussions. Cecile stole a glance at her watch. Four o'clock. Time had flown. "Cecile?"

She glanced down the table. His blue-eyed gaze locked onto hers. "You're going to be handling one of the location segments we're shooting at the Brickyard, so will you please stay behind for a moment?"

"Sure," Cecile said, reopening the folder she'd just closed.

"Super. Everyone, have a great Fourth of July tomorrow and I'll see you in the studio Wednesday morning at seven."

The room erupted in the sound of shuffles and chairs moving as everyone but Cecile exited the room. She remained seated, noting that the door was left open. As the glassed-in room sat in the middle of the production floor, she suddenly felt like a fish in a bowl. Then again, with all of the blinds open, what could Luke do to her here? Anyone walking by could see them.

Maybe he'd just let her stew. Give her the silent treatment. Luke shuffled some papers and closed the file folder. He glanced over at her as if seeing her for the first time. "My office is around the corner. I didn't think you'd appreciate me summoning you in front of everyone else, but I'd rather talk there. Let's go."

She wanted to reply with a glib "Yes, sir" but held her tongue as she stood and followed him. Luke's office was located on the other side of the conference room and the elevators, and she noticed as they approached that his office took up a large section of the building's eastern side.

"Come in," Luke said, reaching to pull the blinds closed as he entered his office. "Take a seat."

He gestured to a pair of leather wingback chairs strategically placed in front of a huge mahogany workstation. Luke's office had three separate spaces: his desk area, a computer production station and a lounge area comprised of couches and a plasma-screen television.

Cecile arched an eyebrow and waited. Patience was a virtue she often didn't have, except when absolutely necessary. She could tell this was one of those times.

"So why'd you do it?" Luke asked simply.

Luke crossed his arms and Cecile could almost hear him mentally counting to ten. He shook his head. He looked great even in unflattering fluorescent light. He edged closer.

Despite the tension in the room, Cecile's body began to hum, proving what she'd had with him wasn't just a temporary infatuation. "I don't like morning-after conversations. They're awkward," she said, rattled that he still affected her.

His blond eyebrow arched in silent dare. "And this isn't?"

"Okay, fine, it is," Cecile conceded. To escape his proximity, she sat down and stared up at him. "Did you know I'd be working for you beforehand? Is that why you picked me up?" she asked.

His classic expression of disbelief said it all. "*I* picked *you* up? *You* made the moves at my apartment."

"You were hitting on me."

He didn't reply, so she pressed forward, slinging a barbed excuse. "As for me, I just had a low moment, some weak resolve. So *did* you know I'd be working here?"

"No," Luke barked, not bothering to hide his irritation at her comment. "I found out yesterday morning. Soon after you left, I opened the file of my new employee and there you were."

And he hadn't thought to call her, to let her know? His decision only made her angrier. While she had left, his discovery that he was her boss had changed things.

"How convenient," Cecile said, her derogatory tone indicating what she thought about that move. "I won't even degrade myself by asking if you'd have called me had I left a number. Not that you couldn't have found my cell phone number in my employment file or at the top of my résumé."

He sat down next to her and leaned back, his body filling the entire chair. He crossed his arms over his chest and waited while she fumed as another minute ticked by.

"Don't we have business? Work to do?" she prodded, impatient for her first day to be over. Her dream job was fast becoming a nightmare roller-coaster ride, one totally out of control.

"We do need to discuss your position," Luke agreed, his calm demeanor infuriating as he agreed with her. He stretched his legs forward and made himself comfortable, crowding her space. Cecile tamped down her temper at his deliberate movement. Luke was clearly letting her know he was master of this moment.

But even worse was that his proximity was drawing from her all the reactions he wanted. She'd grown edgy as her control had slipped. In the mental arena, he'd bested her just by being her boss. In the physical arena, her body *knew* his. It was as if someone had notched up the thermostat, making the temperature in the room skyrocket.

What was it about this man that simply got under her skin? She didn't know if she wanted to flog him or kiss him. Both would get her fired. When she'd met with Allegra this morning, Allegra had made it clear she viewed office romances as grounds for dismissal. At this moment Cecile was grateful Allegra had no idea about Cecile and Luke's past!

For that's what it was. The past.

"I believe we will be able to work together just fine,"

Cecile stressed, determined to retake some ground. "We just need to keep things in perspective and remember that we have a job to do. That's all I'm here for."

"Fine. Then I want to hear your ideas for the Brickyard," Luke said, his business persona dropping quickly into place. "As you know, NASCAR counts more than thirty million women among its fans, and Allegra wants to reach them. She's been invited to start the race and thus has decided to do a series of three NASCAR shows. We've got a tour bus that can double as an on-site interview location that we've managed to get into the infield. Allegra's going to film the driver interview show next week as the first show. We'll be there long before she arrives. She wants two post-race shows."

"Are we staying at the track, like the drivers?" Cecile asked, her composure solid now that Luke had turned his attention to the show. Luke was at ease when discussing business, and Cecile found the change of topic invigorating. This was why she'd come to work on *The Allegra Montana Show.*

"We've booked rooms in a local hotel. We'll have credentials that will let us come and go from just about everywhere at the Brickyard, including some of the drivers' pits."

"Hmm," Cecile said as she processed the information. She'd done many location shoots, but this was NASCAR's Brickyard 400 and, like the Daytona 500, it was a huge race and media event. Indianapolis was three hours from Chicago, and the event would be a perfect place to showcase Allegra to a new audience.

Cecile didn't necessarily follow stock car racing the way she did baseball or hockey, but she'd produced shows before on topics on which she had no prior knowledge. The key was research—and some luck.

But as sleeping with her new boss had proved, Cecile's luck might have run out.

"I read over all the files you sent down before the meeting. Since Allegra has some of the top drivers coming into the studio to talk racing, I was thinking that we should do one of our on-site shows on the drivers' wives."

Luke nodded as if he liked the idea, so Cecile continued, "Our viewers would be interested in what it's like being married to a man who's on the road almost every weekend from mid-February through mid-November. No other professional athlete has that long of a season, and we could put an interesting spin on it. Allegra could dig past the surface glamour and get to the human factor. Romance and racing—it's not all sweet victory."

"I like that," Luke said. "No one else has worded that segment quite that way. That might be very workable."

"Thanks," Cecile said. She found her face flushing like a schoolgirl's as she took a second to bask in his compliment. She shifted, riveting her aloof composure back into place. He had gotten under her skin once; she could not let his charisma sway her again. Especially since she had no desire to be fired before even proving herself.

"I think we should focus on three wives, and not necessarily the wives of the drivers on the kickoff show. I want one who's been married to her husband for several years and one whose marriage is pretty new. The other one could be somewhere in the middle, preferably with kids. I'd like to see a range, the full spectrum."

"Interview separately or alone?" Luke asked.

"Since all the guys are going to be on the show all at once, how about a little feature on each wife? We could include things such as baby pictures, home videos. What they do during the race—do they stay in an air-conditioned skybox, a motor coach or hang out in the pit? And then have Allegra interview them one at a time so that they're all sitting there on stage together by the end."

"I'll ask Set Design what they can come up with. We'd need to piece all this together correctly. I'd like for you to work up some storyboards so we can discuss your ideas later this week. I'll have Research and Talent investigate wives who might be interested in talking to us."

"Okay," she said, realizing she was admiring him. Luke was a dynamo. She'd been waiting a lifetime to work with someone like him. Heck, she'd been waiting a lifetime to fall for someone like him.

Fate had to be mocking her right about now. Right in front of her was Cecile's ideal man, and she couldn't touch him without fast becoming unemployed. Suddenly the idea of not touching him ever again bothered her immensely.

"You okay?" Luke asked as if sensing her conundrum.

"Fine," Cecile said, resolving not to let herself be affected despite her heart's desire for a connection. She'd made a vow to wait for Mr. Right, and here he was, off-limits.

"Susan's got the other on-site show pretty much nailed down. We're going to be investigating the rabid fan. I've seen those storyboards, so let's do lunch Friday. I have an hour between tapings, so I can work you in."

Lunch? With him?

"That will be fine," Cecile said, calming herself quickly and reminding herself that producers often held working lunches. Purely professional.

"I'll have something ready to present." With the meeting almost over, Cecile shifted forward, ready to make her escape. However, she'd have to step across Luke's outstretched legs unless he moved them, which he didn't seem too inclined to do.

"Are we finished?" Cecile prompted.

Luke stared at her for a minute, those blue eyes unblinking. "Yeah," he said in a tone so final Cecile's head turned sharply. "Yeah, we're finished." He drew up his legs and straightened. She rose to her feet, grabbed the file folder she'd set on the side table and headed for the door. Luke remained in place as if deep in thought. She'd reached for the doorknob before his voice had her pausing and turning.

"Cecile?"

Luke was now on his feet, his weight on his left leg. He'd folded his arms across his chest, the movement making his posture read more disappointed than chastising.

"Yes?" she asked, eager to go home and put the day behind her.

"One last thing before you go. I believe you wanted

an answer to your question. It's very simple. While, yes, I could have located your number, you left without a note. I figured that meant *do not disturb* and I don't go where I'm not welcome. Had *you* left a number, I would have called."

"You would have," Cecile stopped herself before she could add *called me*. She would not sound elated or giddy. Despite her body's humming, what they had was over. She had to work with him, and Allegra's warning about fraternization rang in her ear. "You would have to have the last word," Cecile said instead.

"It's my job," Luke said, the easy tone gone. "I'm the boss."

Yes, he was, and as Cecile fled for her office, she realized that was a very big problem indeed.

Chapter Seven

"What do you mean you slept with your boss?" From Kansas City, Tori Adams's voice resounded through the earpiece Cecile wore. "Cecile, you usually have more common sense than I do! Not as much as Lisa or Joann but at least more than me!"

"It was the wedding. The romance, the happiness, the wine," Cecile said, peeling the label of the longneck bottle of beer sitting in front of her. She'd broken down on the way home from work, stopped at a corner store and bought a six-pack of domestic light beer, her first indulgence whenever she needed a pity party. She'd resolved to drink only one, and wine was forbidden, especially since drinking that beverage was what had gotten her into this fix in the first place.

"So you had too much at your sister's wedding and you went to his place," Tori summarized the story she'd just heard.

"In a nutshell," Cecile said, moving about her apartment. Once the maintenance had been completed, she'd moved in without a hitch. "You know, I told myself, don't do anything. Somehow it might bite me. But a few glasses and I was a goner. And he's my boss. He realized it after I'd left and he didn't call me to warn me."

"You said you didn't leave your number."

"So? He grew up next door to Devon. Devon married Elizabeth. How tough is it to find me? He had my résumé! He said something about not going where he wasn't wanted. Typical man, to find an excuse for not being chivalrous."

Instead of answering, Tori asked, "Is he hot?"

"As a summer day," Cecile said. "Blond hair. Blue eyes. Tall. Well, taller than me, and that's saying something. Great body without an inch of fat. Which, of course, I shouldn't know! I have to work with the man, not drool over his six-pack abs."

"I worked with Jeff," Tori pointed out. She'd had an on-and-off-again thing with her boss for over two years. Cecile had been privy to much of the drama, especially whenever Tori thought she'd gotten herself in too deep.

"I don't know," Cecile said. "I've been in stickier spots before, just not personal ones that involved an exchange of bodily fluids."

"Eww," Tori said. "Stop trying to cheapen what happened between you and just own up to it. I'm sure bedding him wasn't simply a clinical act. I bet it was wonderful."

"It was," Cecile said, her fingers automatically pressing her lips, remembering how Luke's mouth had felt on hers. Scintillating.

"Then, whatever you do, don't mock what you two shared in an attempt to make yourself feel better," Tori admonished. "Do you like the guy?"

"Allegra outlined her no-fraternization policy during my meeting with her this morning," Cecile said. "I don't want to lose my job because of Luke. So what happened must remain a secret. And it can't be repeated."

"You didn't answer my question," Tori pointed out. "I didn't ask why you couldn't see him, I asked if you liked him."

Cecile left the bottle of beer on her kitchen counter, hopped off the bar stool, picked up the cell phone and began to pace. "I don't know. He's intriguing. Dynamic."

"Sounds like just the type of man to tame you," Tori observed.

"Tame me? I'm not a wild animal," Cecile protested. "Please."

"No, but you are an unrestrained woman," Tori said. "You live life on your terms, always have. So let's take a minute and consider this from his point of view. Better yet, put yourself in his shoes. You and he share a passionate night. He's older."

"Thirty-five is not old."

"Older than you," Tori continued without missing a beat. "He's wealthy, probably the type women fawn on."

"Well, I did tell you about Loretta and how she hit on him until he said he was my date," Cecile conceded.

"Exactly. He picked you, even wearing that ugly dress you told me about. And you two hit it off in every way possible. Then he wakes up and finds out that you've gone. Poof, vanished without a trace. Heck, if I found out I was your boss, I'd give myself license for some payback, too. You took all his options away by walking out the door without a goodbye. He's not some young twenty-something just out for jollies. I'm guessing he wasn't planning on just one night."

"Oh, come on," Cecile said. "I can buy the part about payback and perhaps wanting some perverse satisfaction at my expense. But I can't fathom that he thought I was worth another go-round."

"He said he would have called."

"He was just fulfilling his need to have the last word, to win the argument."

"I don't believe that's all it is—and I don't even know the guy. I know you. You can convince yourself of anything. But you called me for my advice, so I'm going to give it to you. Apologize to him. Say you're sorry."

"What?" Cecile stopped tracing a path across her living room carpet and froze in front of her picture window. From behind the building that stood directly across the street she could see the slivers of sunset.

"Cecile, he's your boss. Go apologize to the man and tell him you don't usually treat men like pieces of meat and that you were under a great deal of stress with your sister's wedding, moving and starting a new job. He's a guy. They eat this stuff up. He'll be sympathetic and then you can both put what happened behind you. We hate it when guys use us. I'm sure he's the same way about a woman using him. So offer the white flag and move on."

"Is that what you did with Jeff?"

"Jeff and I have so many problems it's not funny. He's not the type to ever settle down. If I didn't work with his family, I'd never know them. He keeps his life compartmentalized. I have my box and I get to come out of it every once in a while. That's why I'm glad to have moved to Kansas City. I had to get a fresh start and a new perspective. Things have been so stressful. And, frankly, I'm turning thirty. We vowed long ago to have it all by age thirty, and, darn it, while I know that's unrealistic, I just don't want to give up trying. So I don't have any more time to spend on something that simply isn't going to be more than it is. I've decided to take action. I signed up for one of those online dating sites."

"You didn't?"

"I really did. It's time for me to get back on the market. I haven't gotten through all the ads yet. Since I was always back and forth between the home office and this one in Kansas City, I've already got a few girlfriends here. Some of us enrolled on the same site. That way we can screen guys who hit on everyone and thus eliminate the losers."

"You never cease to amaze me," Cecile said. "I would never date online. Meeting people in bars and through work has been bad enough."

"Well, you'll have to get back out there eventually."

"Yeah, later. Although I did tell you that Lisa declared that I'm the next one to get married," Cecile said. "Like that's on the horizon."

"You never know," Tori said drily. "Stranger things have happened."

Trying to change the subject, Cecile said, "Have you seen Lisa lately? How does she look?"

"Very happy. I had dinner with her, Mark and Joann last weekend. We all met up in Columbia. Anyone can just glance at her and see how much she's in love and that he's simply gaga over her."

"Good," Cecile said. "I'm so glad she's found the right person."

"Oh, he is. So now you need to find someone so that I can be in your wedding and get those fun maid of honor duties."

"Someday, maybe," Cecile said.

"You know, your sister could probably introduce you to some guys. That hubby of hers has to have some single friends," Tori suggested.

"He does," Cecile said drolly. "Luke."

"Oh, yeah. Well, I'm sure there are others."

"I'll just concentrate on my career. Fate's already laughing at me. And I don't want just another Mr. Right Now."

"You're reforming," Tori said, her tone both surprised and impressed.

"No, I just want a deeper connection," Cecile said. Besides, Luke had put all other men to shame. She didn't even want to contemplate how she was going to find a guy to top him. Luke had rewritten the playbook. He'd made everyone else seem, well, inferior.

"Listen, I should probably get off now before I die of shock that Cecile—the one who we always envied for her Teflon way of protecting her heart—wants something emotional from a man," Tori said. "That and I've got another call coming in."

"No, that's my phone," Cecile said. She glanced at the display. "It's my sister. I'll talk to you later."

"You better. And don't forget to apologize to him. Trust me on this."

"Last time you said that we almost got arrested for jumping in that fountain."

"Ha-ha," Tori said. "But we didn't. So this time do what I say, not as I do." And with that, she hung up, and Cecile clicked over to catch Elizabeth's phone call.

"Hi, Elizabeth."

"Cecile!" Elizabeth's overly excited voice boomed through the earpiece, and Cecile quickly turned down the volume. "How are you? I haven't had a chance to talk to you since the wedding. How's the new job?"

"Great." *I'm working with Luke.*

"Oh, that's wonderful. Listen, I'm arranging a small dinner party for family and friends tomorrow night. Besides ringing in the Fourth of July, we're going to show our wedding photos. Mom and Dad will be there, and I'd love for you to come. Do say you're free."

Cecile had made it one of her goals to spend more time with her sister now that they both lived in Chicago.

"It's my first big party in my new house," Elizabeth added helpfully.

"I'll be there," Cecile said.

"That's wonderful," Elizabeth said. "I'm glad you're back in town. I've missed you and want for us to get closer."

"I'd like that, too," Cecile said.

"I'm glad. Devon and I have baseball season tickets, and tomorrow when you come over I want you to pick out a game that you'll go to with us."

"Okay," Cecile said, flattered. Everyone knew how sports-crazy she was, especially about her hometown teams. She had a feeling Dr. Devon Pinewood probably had some pretty decent seats.

"So bring your calendar tomorrow night. And I have some gossip for you. Luke Shaw asked about you last night when Devon and I had him over for dinner."

"He asked only because he's my boss."

"What? You work for him? I'd forgotten. He does work for a talk show, doesn't he? So you both work on the same show?"

"We do. I found out today."

"Well, that makes things convenient. He lives near you, so drive out here with him. He said yes yesterday."

Cecile bristled. One more thing Luke had failed to mention.

"Don't matchmake," Cecile heard herself say. "Allegra has a no-fraternization policy, and I don't need to get fired. I'll drive myself out to your place. Just give me directions."

"Cecile, a friend of my husband's is a friend of yours, and a girl can never have too many friends. You won't get fired for that. I'll call Luke and call you back. Ciao!"

"Wait!" Cecile began, but it was already too late as Elizabeth had hung up. "Bye to you, too," Cecile said grumpily. She snapped the phone closed and glanced around her now-dark twenty-seventh floor apartment. Somehow during the conversations she'd sat on the couch, the cell phone resting in the palm of her hand.

She removed the earpiece from her ear, set both it and the phone on the coffee table and stared into space. She'd hardly settled in Chicago and already life was crazy. Had it been like this in New York City? She'd been working 24-7, constantly in motion as if living her life in fast-forward.

But this sensation was different. She wasn't so much moving fast as moving out of control. Fate had simply taken her life and upended it like a bowl of cherries into her lap. What a mess.

She stood and moved into the kitchen, deciding that some dinner was in order. She hadn't drank much of her beer and she poured out the remnants. The refrigerator provided slim pickings, so she grabbed the leftover chicken from the night before and popped the container into the microwave.

As she pressed start, her cell phone rang again. She picked up the phone, reading a Chicago area code but not recognizing the number. Sighing, she flipped open the phone to connect the call. "Hello?"

"Hi, gorgeous."

Luke. She should have guessed. "Isn't it sexual harassment for you to call me gorgeous?" she asked, struggling for the control he'd pulled out from under her like a rug.

"Would you rather me call you ugly?" he countered easily and she could almost picture the cheeky smile. Before she could answer, he continued. "Didn't think so. Anyway, 'hi, gorgeous' just had a better ring to it. I hear you're my date tomorrow night."

Her heart fluttered.

"I am not your date. I can drive myself to Elizabeth and Devon's just fine. I've driven in New York City. Chicago is a drive in the country compared to Manhattan or Brooklyn. So no, thanks."

There was only a second of silence before he countered with, "Still, you're not that far from me and I go past your building when headed west. Not out of my way at all."

"How convenient," Cecile said, irritated at how smoothly Luke could operate. "You couldn't find my phone number but you can find my apartment. Wouldn't this count as fraternization?"

"No, and just so you know, after I discovered you were my new AP, I told Allegra this morning that my best friend married your sister and we'd met at the wedding."

"You told her that? And you didn't tell me?"

"I didn't think I needed to. I know Allegra, and letting her know we'd met immediately defuses the situation. She's a very up-front person."

"You really do take care of everything, don't you?" Cecile asked. No wonder Allegra had outlined her fraternization policy so fully. She was probably worried Cecile might decide to hit on Luke!

"So what time shall I come get you?" Luke asked. "I've been told we're to feel free to come out around noon and use the pool."

She'd seen him naked. Seeing him in a swimsuit

would bring back images best forgotten…. "I try not to date my coworkers and I have a pool here that I can use if I want to swim."

"Of course you do," Luke said, not missing a beat. "And I bet with your fair skin you also try to stay out of the sun."

"I turn red, not tan. Doesn't match my hair," Cecile said. "So I'll drive out later."

"Cecile, give up. I will win this. Stop being stubborn and just say yes. What impression would Elizabeth and Devon get if we arrive separately? Do you want them to suspect something happened between us and that's why we can't be in the same car?"

"Fine." He'd trapped her. No man had ever gotten the upper hand with her the way Luke did. Just as at the wedding reception, the man made her want to throw caution to the wind. Trapped in a car with him, they'd talk. She'd probably find out he was even more perfect for her. Her defenses would crumble and she'd do something foolish. Like jump all over him. And get fired.

"Then the later we arrive is best if I'm stuck going with you."

"Such enthusiasm," Luke said. "We'll have a good time. We had one before."

"I'm trying to forget that."

"I'm not," he said simply. "It was a great night. I think it's well worth remembering. To forget would cheapen what we shared."

His logic made sense, but she couldn't let the moment become more than it was. Too much was at stake. "This isn't a game. I want you to stop flirting with me. We have to be professional and work together."

"I wasn't aware I was flirting," Luke said.

"Yeah, and I own the title to the Brooklyn Bridge and can sell it to you cheap."

"You wound me," Luke parried easily. "But to no avail. I'm driving you tomorrow and I'll pick you up at four."

"Fine," Cecile said, a smile slipping across her face. The man was as tenacious as a bulldog. Despite herself, she liked the sensations he elicited. Then again, she often liked things that were bad for her. Like ice cream. Delicious. Tasty. Forbidden from her diet since indulging meant she had to run extra laps. Of course, that didn't mean she didn't crave it every day. "I'm at One West Superior. I'll meet you in the lobby."

"That's fine," Luke said. "You can keep your apartment number a secret. I don't need to see the inside."

He'd twisted her words again. "That's not it. Although I've unpacked everything, it's still a mess," Cecile admitted.

"I drive a dark blue Monte Carlo," Luke said. "Watch for me."

"I'll do that," Cecile said.

"Then I'll see you at four," Luke said. "And, Cecile?"

"Yes?"

"Stop worrying. You already know I don't bite."

And with that, Luke hung up the phone. Cecile snapped hers closed, the quick noise not enough to soothe her frustration. The man was infuriating! He'd gotten the last word—again! He was one of those men

101

who she couldn't control. In fact, he made *her* spin out of control, as if she were on a carnival ride. He was—

Her equal.

She fell against the sofa with a muted thump, her back sinking into the soft cushions. She'd never met a man who could match her personality, who could be the yin to her yang. But Luke was the man who could. He got the last word. He made her speechless. He'd loved her body and brought her places no man had ever been able to take her. He challenged her mind.

And he was her boss. Life was so unfair.

Cecile now understood exactly what Tori meant by saying that Cecile's best course of action was to apologize. If Cecile herself was experiencing this massive frustration because of finding such a great guy and being forbidden to do anything about it, then what was Luke going through? Perhaps much worse. Cecile had left him. She'd walked out, ending the night on her terms. She'd given little thought to the consequences of those actions until they'd come back to haunt her.

Luke had said that he'd planned to call her. Read between the lines: he'd admitted that the specialness she'd experienced that night hadn't been one-sided. He'd felt it, too. He'd wanted more. He'd chosen her.

And she'd left, dashing any hopes before they could begin. Now it was too late. They worked together. They could only be friends.

They could never be more unless one of them quit or got fired. Not an option. Whereas men had often come and gone, her career had been the one stalwart, her one sanctuary. She was good at what she did, and this was one area in which she refused to compromise.

Cecile reached over and turned on the lamp. Light flooded the room, chasing away the darkness. She rose to her feet, remembering that she'd forgotten about the chicken she'd put in the microwave. She wasn't in the mood for it anyway.

Living in New York had taught her that walking cleared her head. Cecile changed into some tennis shoes, tucked her front door key, phone and some cash into her pants pocket and headed for the elevator. She'd get some dinner while she was out and hopefully be able to figure out exactly what to do about Luke.

LUKE ARRIVED PROMPTLY at four. Last night, before he'd told her what he drove, she would have pegged him for a two-seater-sports-car kind of guy. Maybe something low-slung and foreign. But once again Luke defied her pigeonholing. The inside of the car was luxurious but understated. He handled the car easily, accelerating quickly to the speed limit once on the highway. Before long they'd be in Barrington, pulling up to the three-story traditional house that Elizabeth and Devon had purchased on a tree-lined street. Already several other cars were parked in the circular driveway.

"I guess we're not the first ones here," Cecile said lamely. Conversation in the car on the drive out had been pretty stilted. They'd mainly ignored each other and listened to National Public Radio, the tension between them obvious. Chemistry still hummed beneath the surface like sweet torture, making Cecile feel like a kid on a diet who was standing outside a bakery store window.

"A lot of other people probably came early to swim," Luke said as he turned off the engine and removed the key from the ignition. "Wait there and I'll get your door."

"I've got it, thanks," Cecile said, opening her door at the same time he opened his. She didn't want to risk feeling his touch on hers, for that would fuel memories best left dormant.

She climbed out of the car and reached for the bottle of wine she'd brought as a housewarming present.

Elizabeth opened the front door and greeted Cecile with a warm hug. She hugged Luke, as well, and ushered them both inside. "Everyone's out back on the patio," she said, leading them through the immaculately decorated house. "Wait until you see our backyard. It's my favorite area."

"Your home is lovely," Cecile said automatically, for a minute fighting the twinge of jealousy. Her younger sister had already achieved the house, the man and the… Out of the corner of her eye Cecile saw a cat walk nonchalantly into another room. And the cat, Cecile amended. As it had at the wedding, a bit of envy consumed her and she stole a glance at Luke.

They passed through the kitchen with its granite countertops and Elizabeth put down the bottle of wine. "We set up the bar outside," she said. She led them through a hearth room and out onto a huge landscaped patio. As had always been her family's tradition for any large event, a professional bartender served drinks in the corner. Elizabeth waved at Devon, who barbecued on a huge outdoor grill.

"What do you want to drink?" Luke asked Cecile as Elizabeth went to speak with her husband for a moment.

"Iced tea is fine," Cecile said. As Luke moved toward the bar, she could hear people splashing in the pool. A glance down the stone patio revealed a huge inground pool just about fifteen feet away. She also saw her mother seated under a large umbrella and headed over.

"Hi, honey, I'm so glad you could make it." Clarann Duletsky rose from a nearby lounge chair and gave her daughter a brief hug. "It means a lot to your sister that you're here. I know you two have never really been close."

"We're both trying, Mom," Cecile said. Dark haired like Elizabeth, her mother wore a gauzy shirt over her one-piece swimsuit. Clarann was a tall woman and as she settled back down, she patted the end of the cushioned lounger. "I've been out here for way too long. Sit down and talk to me for a few moments before I go inside and change for dinner. How was your first day on the job? Elizabeth tells me you're working for Luke?"

"I am."

"Oh, that's wonderful. Devon's mom regaled me over lunch with all of Luke's accomplishments. You're lucky to be working for him. Amanda said he's very good."

"He is," Cecile said, not loving the vein of the conversation. Her sister had insisted she ride with him, now her mother was singing his praises. Was everyone trying to matchmake?

"Your iced tea," Luke said, approaching. He held out the glass and Cecile reached up to take it from him.

"Thanks."

He wiped the condensation on his khaki shorts before reaching to shake Clarann's fingers in a light handshake. "Good to see you again, Clarann."

"Likewise," Clarann said. "Amanda's been telling me all about your work on *The Allegra Montana Show*."

"Amanda's like my second mom. She loves to brag and make a big deal out of nothing," Luke insisted modestly.

"Well, I'm delighted that you're going to be working with Cecile here. She's a great producer."

"I agree. We'll make a good team." Luke said the last words with a direct glance at Cecile. She flushed for a moment, and then Luke was making his excuses and moving off to say hello to Devon.

Clarann's gaze followed Luke's backside for a moment before she swung her attention back to her daughter. "You really shouldn't let that one get away."

"Mom," Cecile protested, almost sputtering the sip of iced tea she'd just taken. "Luke and I work together. We're colleagues, that's all. Allegra has a no-fraternization policy, just so you know. And since when did you turn all marriage-minded?"

"I've mellowed as the years have gone by. Your sister certainly seems happy."

"So am I. You always taught me to be independent

and wait for the right person. Don't you dare tell me that my clock's ticking."

Clarann sighed. "Life's just too short not to have everything."

"I know that," Cecile said. "But I'm not going to settle. At least Elizabeth's happy."

"She is. I just want to see you the same way. And I do hope the two of you grow closer now that you're back."

"I hope so, too. It's been hard. I've been gone and I only see her at family holidays. We e-mail jokes, but we don't chat on the phone."

"The age difference thing always was a problem between you two, and you're as different as oil and water—she played with dolls, you cut off all their hair. But she's happy. And life is short. To make any relationship work, you have to compromise. You're very stubborn. The question is whether the thing you fight over is something you value or can live with. I just want you to be happy. Are you really happy?"

Cecile always hated it when her mother turned philosophical and then began to pry. "Mom, let's not have this discussion now. I love my career. I'm delighted to be back in Chicago. So, yes, I'm happy."

"But having someone there is one of the best things in life," her mother said.

"Mom," Cecile protested. This conversation was quickly getting too personal and a bit uncomfortable. Sure, she was happy with her career, but, yes, she was disappointed she didn't yet have everything she'd vowed to have. But she wasn't going to tell that to her mother.

Cecile had always been one to keep the brave face and she refused to change now and admit weakness.

So instead she glanced at her drink. She'd just about drained all the iced tea. She took a big gulp. If she finished it quickly, she could use getting a refill as an excuse to escape.

"I need to get more iced tea," Cecile said. "And you said you wanted to change clothes. It looks like Devon's done on the barbecue. He's taking a huge platter inside the screened porch."

"Yes, I suppose it's that time," Clarann said. She adjusted her chair and both women stood.

"I'll see you at dinner," Cecile said. As her mother went inside, Cecile glanced around. She didn't see her dad. Knowing him, he'd escaped inside and had parked himself in front of the television. Maybe she should join him.

"We're city people," a deep voice whispered in her ear. Cecile closed her eyes as Luke's warm breath tickled her ear. "Just breathe and relax. The air out here's no different from when we were kids."

Her eyes flew open. "Just stop. I am not freaking out." Okay, maybe she was. The city's hustle and busyness provided solace. You were never alone. Suburbia was too, well, couple-y. "You do not need to rescue me."

"I never said I was," Luke pointed out. "I rescued you once and look how badly that turned out."

"Our night together wasn't that bad," Cecile said automatically.

"No, it wasn't," he agreed. "And I'm glad you finally

admit it and expose my lie. Despite what happened afterward, I would not trade that night."

He'd given her the perfect opportunity, and Tori's words resounded in Cecile's head. *Just apologize.* She stepped closer, into his space. Were her hands sweaty or was it from the condensation on the empty glass? Luke waited, sensing she had something to tell him. Now all Cecile had to do was open her mouth and say...

"Dinner's inside." Elizabeth's voice rang clearly across the patio. "Come and get it while it's hot."

"I guess we should go eat," Cecile said. She shook the glass and the ice cubes rattled. "I also need to get a refill. Shall I get you anything while I'm at the bar?"

Luke held up a longneck bottle of beer that was still half-full. "I'm good. This is my one and only indulgence for the evening, as I'm driving. I'll meet you by the food. How about we sit at that table over there?"

"I thought I might eat with my parents," Cecile said. "Since this isn't a date." The last thing she wanted to do was fuel more rumors that she and Luke were together.

"Suit yourself," Luke said. "Don't let me keep you."

Cecile watched as he strode onto the screened porch, where the food had been set up buffet-style. She winced. So much for apologizing. So much for doing anything right. Once again she'd terribly blown things with Luke. Her stars must be crossed or something.

Worse, as Luke struck up conversation with the cute brunette next to him in line, Cecile experienced an angry pang. No. He made the green-eyed monster inside her flare, just as he had at the wedding reception. She couldn't let herself care that much. And Luke Shaw was off-limits. She couldn't have him.

So why did she want him so badly?

Chapter Eight

"Hey, Cecile, I see you and Luke are getting along great." A movement to Cecile's left indicated that her sister had decided to join Cecile at the table. Elizabeth set down a plate of food and a large glass of clear soda. "So where is he?"

"He went to get some food. He got this plate for me." After her earlier comments, the gesture had surprised her.

"That's Luke for you," Elizabeth said. Her long dark hair was pulled back into a ponytail, and she had a glow about her that didn't come from her daily run or from weekend golf and tennis games. "Luke's the nicest guy I know. When I had some doubts about Devon, he was the voice of reason that I really needed to hear."

That admission caught Cecile off guard. "You had doubts about Devon?"

Elizabeth nodded. "Every woman has doubts about the man she falls in love with. I mean, marriage is a lifetime commitment. How do you know that someone better isn't just around the corner?"

"I don't know," Cecile said, finding it strangely comfortable to be sharing confidences with her sister. "I thought Eric was the one, which is why we moved in together, but that didn't even work out. I'm certainly not a poster girl for love and happily ever after. I don't want to be wrong again."

"See, that's what I mean," Elizabeth said. "Devon's older than I am. He's established. And four years ago he picked me? That's just crazy. I was in college. I'm nine-to-five and his job means erratic schedules. We're completely opposite in many areas, sort of like you and me, but for some reason our relationship works. I can say I love him with all my heart, white tube socks, snoring and all."

"White tube socks?"

"Devon's an orthopedic surgeon. He's rabid about wearing these special white tube socks everywhere he goes. That's my husband—all about comfort even if it makes him seem like he has no fashion sense."

"Did I just hear my name?" Devon approached, followed by Luke. Both carried plates of food in their hands.

"I was telling Cecile about your tube socks," Elizabeth said. She turned her face up, and Devon dropped a quick kiss on her lips before settling himself in the chair next to her. Cecile averted her gaze from the personal moment just in time to catch Luke pulling out the chair inches to her left. Her mother had joined her father inside.

"Those socks are legendary," Luke said as he sat down. "He even convinced me to try them a few times, but I just can't get into wearing them, especially with shorts."

"Probably wise," Elizabeth said. "You'd run off all your admirers. It takes a special woman to love a man in white tube socks."

"I'd say," Devon said.

Elizabeth picked up her fork. "So, Luke, what's up next on your taping schedule?"

"Tons of things," Luke said as he began to outline some of the guests that Allegra had booked on her show. While Luke talked, Cecile had the opportunity to view him in yet another new situation. He and Devon obviously shared a close bond, one Cecile hadn't really been able to see up close until now. The wedding had been way too busy and frazzling and then, of course, she'd been way too enamored with Luke to study him in depth.

Now she watched him interact, analyzing his movements as she'd do with a potential interviewee. She observed how, when he held his fork in his right hand, his pinky curled back toward his palm. A lump formed in her throat. She was powerfully attracted to him, and the chemistry coursing its way through her body was quite frankly making her uncomfortable.

"Have you been sailing much this summer, Luke?" Elizabeth asked.

"Not nearly as much as I'd like," he said. "I got some in during the June break, but oftentimes the weather was bad."

"We did have a stormy June," Elizabeth said.

"And since then, Allegra's show really has had me pretty tied up."

"Well, let me know when you're going next. I want to get back out on the water before we have kids," Elizabeth said.

"You're pregnant?" Cecile asked.

"Not yet but hopefully soon," she said. She rattled her glass. "That's why I'm forgoing anything but soda. We're trying."

"Congrats," Cecile said. She'd known this, but to hear Elizabeth voice it so plainly made Cecile feel, well, outdated. As if her mother was correct and life was passing Cecile by.

"How about weekend after next?" Luke suggested. "The weather is supposed to be gorgeous for the next two weeks. Next weekend I'm going to be in Joliet, at the Chicagoland 400 doing some background research, but my schedule's free after that."

He was? Cecile hadn't known that. She frowned. Would his research affect her Brickyard segment? She had no idea. Once again, more information she lacked.

"I'd love that," Elizabeth said. She glanced at Devon.

"I'm not on call until the end of the month," he said. "My weekends are my own until then."

"Excellent," Elizabeth said, turning her attention to her sister. "Make sure you mark it on your calendar. You'll love Luke's boat. It's huge."

"You can live on the boat for a few days," Devon explained. "Back in our younger and irresponsible days we once took a summer off and traveled the entire Lake Michigan coastline."

"Say you'll go with us, Cecile," Elizabeth encouraged.

Was she going to have a choice, especially given her resolution to become closer to Elizabeth? "I'll look at my calendar and see what I can do," Cecile promised, grateful her mother decided at that moment to stop by the table. Clarann's arrival gave Cecile a break to finish what food she hadn't eaten and remove herself from the conversation and head to the bar, the safest place she could think of to retreat to aside from the bathroom. Luke's presence in her life rattled her, and she couldn't stop her mind from thinking about him.

If he was Mr. Right, then fate was cruel since she worked with him. Either that or—she had to at least consider the possibility—maybe fate was telling Cecile that she wasn't ready to have an emotional commitment. That she needed to relax.

She'd reached the bar, and the guy tending gave her a smile. He was a nice piece of eye candy, decked out in a black T-shirt, black jeans and a silver name badge. "What can I get you?" Chuck asked.

"What I'd like isn't possible," Cecile said, wondering what was it about bartenders that made them hear more confessions than priests. "So how about some more iced tea?"

"Want anything with it?" he asked, his grin easy and his tone light as he took the empty glass from her hand and discarded it.

She shook her head and smiled at his easy flirtation. He probably made this easy banter with everyone, and pre-Luke she might have indulged in some harmless conversation. "Not this time."

"Too bad." Chuck reached for a fresh plastic cup and began pouring. "Let me know if you change your mind or need anything else."

What she needed she couldn't have. "I will," she said as she took the tea he held out. As he turned to greet the next guest, she stepped away and strode back toward the table using a roundabout way.

"There you are," Luke said as he appeared in her path. "Elizabeth wants to start the slide show soon." He eyed her glass. "I would have gotten that for you."

"Thanks, but I had it," she said.

"I'm sure you did," Luke said, his blue eyes narrowing. Cecile stared at him strangely.

"What's gotten into you?" she asked.

"You have."

"Please," Cecile said sarcastically. She'd taken a route that went past the pool, and no one was around to offer welcome interference.

"Yes, please," Luke said, stepping into her space as she tried to move around him. "You've pushed me far enough tonight and I'd prefer it stop."

"I don't know what you're talking about," she said testily.

Luke arched an eyebrow. "This. Us. The chemistry that's still here raging between us. The clench in my gut when I saw the bartender hit on you."

"He probably hits on everyone," Cecile said, a slight thrill shooting through her. Could Luke possibly be jealous? That would at least make them even.

"Perhaps, but you shouldn't make a habit of picking

up guys at your sister's events—unless, of course, it's the same guy."

"You're not the boss of me," Cecile said, grasping for the first thing that came to mind, no matter how weak. Already her body was reacting, desiring his.

"Oh, yes, Cecile, but I am," Luke said. He reached forward and removed the glass from her hand. Then he snaked the other hand behind her neck and drew her to him. "Perhaps it's time to prove it."

And with that he lowered his lips to hers.

IT'S ABOUT TIME! Luke thought fuzzily as his mouth plundered hers. He'd wanted to touch her that morning after the wedding reception, but she'd vanished. Finding out he was her boss had been hell. But none of that mattered the moment he held her again. Like she had been that night, she was his woman. He'd imprinted himself on her and her body immediately flared to life and responded.

She still wanted him. There was no doubt about that. He could already feel her body's reaction to their deepening kiss.

It was a kiss he wanted to have last forever. He might be able to make Cecile give physically, but he wanted it all. No matter what the risk.

So as hard as it was to do, he pulled away from her. Her eyes widened and she stared at him. It had been one tiny moment, but that kiss had shaken both of them to the core.

She planted her hands on her hips, and he worked to soothe her. "I'm not trying to tease. But we need to talk,"

Luke said simply. "What's happening between us isn't going to go away. What are we going to do about it?"

"I don't know," Cecile said. "Allegra told me about her no-fraternization policy. I can't lose this job. I've worked too hard to get something like this. Allegra's career is on the upswing."

"Believe me, I understand that. I'd prefer not to lose mine either. There aren't too many places left in Chicago I could go without taking a pay cut or a step down," Luke said.

He paused, carefully choosing his words. Any relationship, even a work-only one, depended on how he handled the next few minutes. "Allegra's main concern is for her studio to run smoothly. That leaves us two choices. We can either explore this thing between us and keep it secret from everyone or we can agree to stay away from each other. Personally, I'd like to explore this."

"I'm not good at keeping secrets," Cecile said. "Of my four friends, I'm the one who's the journalist. It's my job to spill the news, not hide it."

"Tell me about your friends," Luke said, curious. "I've only met your sister."

"The four of us met when we joined Rho Sigma Gamma. We call ourselves the Roses. Tori's like me. We used to get into all sorts of trouble together. She's the West Coast supervisor for Wright Solutions, and she just relocated to Kansas City last week."

Luke nodded. "My dad's company uses their software and computer servers. They also built his network. So you've been friends since college?"

"Yes. We pledged together and have been tight ever since. We share all our secrets."

"So have you told them about me?" Luke asked, his question more curiosity than prying.

"A few things," Cecile admitted. "And only to Tori. She's having a relationship with her boss, so she definitely understands what I'm going through, only their company doesn't have a no-fraternization policy. Joann's married with three kids, and I haven't had a chance to get a hold of her yet. She's at the Lake of the Ozarks for the holiday. Lisa's there, too—she's the one who called me at Elizabeth's wedding. I'll be her maid of honor when she marries Mark, Joann's twin brother. It's kind of strange how fate works. She hated him at first."

He was seeing another side to Cecile, one that cared deeply. "You sound like you miss them."

"Every day. We all had such a great time in school, dreaming and scheming. I'm closer to them than I am to Elizabeth, which I guess sounds pathetic since Elizabeth's my sister. She was one of the reasons why I worked so hard to get a job with Allegra. I wanted to come home, maybe build some bridges."

"Which is very admirable," Luke said. He eased the iced tea back into her hand and watched as she took a long drink. Her neck moved and he remembered planting kisses there.

"You know," he said, trying to take his mind off kissing her, "maybe Lisa and Mark's situation isn't so strange. One of the first shows I produced for Allegra was on what makes people fall in love. We discovered that many people who meet their true match are often first repelled by that person. It's not instantaneous combustion but rather a catfight as the couple realizes that they have to cede themselves to the other person. Love isn't about finding an instant soul mate so much as creating one."

"Is that the advice you gave Elizabeth?" Cecile asked. "She said you spoke to her about Devon."

"I did, but that wasn't it. She loves Devon, but marriage is the whole package. She was a bit afraid she couldn't handle being married to a doctor, especially being so much younger than he is. Marriage is a work in progress, at least that's what my parents say, and they've always had what it takes, although it's not been always perfect. I told your sister to hang in there, especially if she believed Devon was worth it. She did, for here we are."

"So do you want it?" Cecile asked.

"What? Marriage? Of course. Doesn't everybody?" Luke asked. He laughed it off, not wanting to reveal how close to the truth she'd actually come. Of course he wanted it. Scary thing was, he could see himself married to her, even though they'd just met.

Luke knew there was something incredible between him and Cecile. Yet he couldn't even get her to go out with him again. Not that he was going to give up easily.

"So," he asked. "Don't you believe everyone wants to be happily married?"

"You know, I wish I could say yes," Cecile said, but

she just wasn't sure. Perhaps it was her failure with Eric. Perhaps it was just the work she did.

"I did a show on once-burned, twice-shy adults that showed there are those who are just as happy and content to be single for the rest of their days. And you can't discount there are those bachelors out there who've never married and they're still living full, successful lives. Like you."

"I suppose," Luke said. "But I've never ruled out getting married, eventually moving to the suburbs and having a houseful of kids and a dog or two."

"Then why haven't you?" Cecile said, sipping more of her iced tea. The glass was a welcome weight in her hand, providing a sense of security. His kiss had rattled her, showing she still wanted him physically. More and more she was becoming convinced that she didn't want to resist Luke, no matter the consequences.

"I haven't met the right person," he said. "And if I do believe I might have found her, there's always something that causes the relationship to self-destruct, something that's proved me wrong."

"I can understand that since it sounds a lot like what happens to me. Tell me, Luke, have you ever really been in love?"

"Have you?" he countered easily.

"Yes, once." Cecile admitted, her brow creasing as she thought of that relationship. "Or at least I thought I was. It didn't work out between us even though we tried the living-together thing. I'm not very good at making the right choices."

And that is the main reason I walked out on you that morning and am living with the regret now. I should have stayed. Now I have no choice but to go.

"Well, that's the same with me—except for the day I met you," Luke said easily, but his voice sounded as if it had caught on something, for he coughed. "Sorry. That probably sounded like an attack."

"It's fine. This is an awkward topic anyway and we should be getting inside to watch the wedding photos. Elizabeth wanted to show them before it got dark."

As if emphasizing the time, the sun dipped below the horizon, casting a yellowish-red glow across the sky.

"We'll continue this later," Luke said.

They probably would, Cecile thought as they walked back toward the house. He'd never answered her question about being in love, and as they reached the party, the moment to ask had passed.

As for what to do about him, she couldn't indulge. Not when her job was at stake. When she'd come to Chicago she'd been determined to plant herself for a while. She refused to be ousted by the end of the week. She had no idea how to tell him for she knew he'd be disappointed. When she and Luke began the long drive back to the city and Cecile had the opportunity to ask, she didn't. Instead she glanced at the dashboard, trying to figure out what to say. Ten o'clock. They both had to be on the set by seven for the filming of two shows, so Cecile asked Luke a question about the schedule.

"Susan's in charge of the first one, so I want you to watch what she does and then visit Postproduction to see how the footage gets pieced together. Allegra has a very specific style and you should catch on quick," Luke said.

"Thanks," Cecile said as Luke turned onto the highway.

"For what?" Luke asked.

"For believing I could do this job," Cecile replied.

He glanced at her. "Your credentials are fine. I have no doubt you'll do a fantastic job. It's the rest of it I'm worried about."

"Worried? About what?"

"About what choice you and I have to make. The decision we haven't yet made."

"Oh, that," Cecile said. She'd been trying to avoid the inevitable. Imagining any possibility where she and Luke could be together and not compromise their careers was tempting.

Just being around him made her act in the most erratic ways. He'd thrown a wrench into her well-oiled world. He was, as Tori said, just the type of man to tame her, to make her consider the art of compromise and the benefits of settling down. But she wasn't good with secrets.

"I think it'll be best if we just act totally professional at work," she told him.

"Okay," Luke said slowly.

"So choice B. We ignore what happened between us."

He was silent for a moment, so Cecile said, "Are you all right with that?"

"Not really," Luke admitted, confirming what she'd suspected. "I'm just trying to figure out what words to use. I guess I should come clean. I should tell you that I'd like to see you spread out underneath me again. That

I want to watch you when you close your eyes and your mouth drops open at the very point you go over the edge. I should probably admit I'm finding it quite frustrating to be around you. You're driving me crazy, being just out of reach and I'm unable to do anything about it."

"Oh, please," Cecile said, crossing and uncrossing her legs at what he was saying. He was inches away from her and his words had turned on the heat, making her feel reckless. She struggled for control and her words came out glib. "This is silly. And if you really think that way, maybe you should come up into my apartment tonight and we'll get this out of our system once and for all."

"As much as the offer is tempting to come back and drive you senseless, I'll pass," Luke said, his knuckles white on the steering wheel. "I'd rather not ruin the illusion or my fantasies. I'd like option A, but I won't push you. So I'll see you in the morning." They'd reached her apartment and he drew up alongside the curb.

"That's it?" Not that she really wanted him to come up and make her…oh, yes, senseless. Okay, after that kiss earlier, she definitely wanted just that. But she couldn't lose her job. While there were other studios in town, other than Oprah's, none were as high caliber. That meant option B, not A, where they indulged in a clandestine romance. Fate was already mocking her. She couldn't risk tempting it again.

And what was this ruining-the-illusion stuff?

But Luke had unlocked the car door, and Cecile decided not to get into it with him. What was the point if they were going to pretend the previous night had never happened and ignore each other from here forward?

Soon enough the chemistry would die, right? They'd each move on, become simply coworkers. She said her goodbyes and within minutes found herself pacing her living room floor as she continued to try to analyze the situation from all angles. Then she gave up. Analyzing was something Lisa would do. Cecile was more of a seat-of-her-pants type of girl who wore her emotions on her sleeve.

Option B wasn't going to work well for her. She'd developed feelings for Luke and she wasn't necessarily good at squashing those. But squash she would. She couldn't risk getting fired. She couldn't risk falling in love and finding out that she wasn't what Luke wanted after all. She'd made her choice. She'd live with it.

Whether she liked it or not.

Chapter Nine

Cecile didn't have much time to contemplate her feelings for Luke or the choice she'd made as, once the next morning arrived, work took over. In fact, except for staff meetings and the stage directions she heard over her headpiece, she didn't have any direct contact with Luke until their lunch on Friday.

And as that moment approached, her concentration lapsed. She bumped into a camera stand. Another time, she forgot her notes and had to call Janice and have her bring them down to the set. The man had rattled her nerves, and Cecile was amazed how aware of him she was, especially now that she'd turned him down and he'd embraced option B full force.

Once, she'd even been pressed up against him in a crowded elevator following a staff meeting. It was the most difficult—and intense—half minute she'd spent with any man. Thankfully everyone else had been oblivious to the growing ache in her heart each time she came in contact with Luke. Option B was not pleasant, and three days later the chemistry and the longing were stronger than ever.

Her watch read ten fifty-five, and she'd be meeting him for lunch in five minutes. She'd finished the storyboards and patted her portfolio as she made her way to his office. Luke's assistant had sent an e-mail this morning indicating that lunch would be held there.

Although when she arrived, she discovered they wouldn't be eating alone. Susan and Matt were already in the room, tearing into the box lunches they'd each grabbed from the greenroom.

"I brought you a turkey club," Susan said, gesturing to a paperboard box. "Will that work?"

"Sounds fine," Cecile said. She set the portfolio next to a chair and took the box that Susan indicated. "What's up?"

"This is the only opportunity Luke's got to discuss the upcoming segments. Allegra decided that she definitely wants some background that we've filmed ourselves before she has the drivers into the studio. So we're heading to Chicagoland Speedway tonight to get some shots of our guests. Ricky's also going the moment he finishes filming this afternoon."

"Okay," Cecile said slowly as she unwrapped her sandwich. Inside the container was a can of soda, a bag of chips, a deli sandwich and a gourmet cookie.

"It's going to be a crazy weekend," Susan said. "We'll travel with four two-man film crews so that we can follow our guys around and locate some rabid fans."

"We'll shoot pieces on our drivers on Saturday," Matt

said. "Whatever race footage we want we'll just get from other media outlets."

"Research also came back with about ten wives willing to be interviewed, so I figured you could use the time to narrow down which ones we should go with," Susan added.

"I have those storyboards all worked up," Cecile said, a bit of a frown on her face. She was going on-site as well? Talk about being left in the dark. She remembered Luke discussing his trip with Devon and Elizabeth. He'd probably just assumed she'd known.

"I have my storyboards on the die-hard fan," Susan said and Cecile focused. "Can I see yours?"

"Sure," Cecile said, reaching down and passing her case over so that Susan could open it up and study the drawings.

"Where's Luke?" Cecile asked. She'd managed to make a dent in her lunch and he was still a no-show.

"He sometimes runs late on days we film," Susan said. "Those final production meetings can run longer."

"Gotcha," Cecile said, and she ate her sandwich while studying the storyboards Susan had developed. "I like this concept. I didn't know that fans traveled from venue to venue."

"Oh, yes. They'll stand in line for hours to get autographs and literally eat, breathe and sleep this sport. They clothe themselves in apparel with their favorite driver's number. They decorate their campers with cardboard cutouts, flags and even blow-up swimming pools."

"It's wild," Matt said.

"It's a big industry," Susan said. "Found this in this women's magazine." She dug in her bag and pulled out an advertisement.

Cecile glanced at it. She really wasn't into NASCAR but had to admit that that one driver looked pretty darn good wearing a pair of Wranglers.

Although, the driver didn't hold a candle to Luke. Luke had been in jeans all week, and Cecile had to admit that she'd found her gaze straying in his direction more than once when she didn't believe anyone else was watching. Once or twice he'd caught her staring, and Cecile had quickly glanced away.

"Great. You're all here," the man in question said in greeting as he finally entered his office, a half-eaten sandwich in his right hand.

Cecile swallowed her sip of soda, hard. Not only was Luke sexy but also having worked with him for four days, Cecile admired his work ethic and drive.

Yesterday Cecile had watched him coach a reluctant guest into revealing some pretty emotional secrets about her childhood, cementing a segment that, when it aired, would show that the effects of child abuse lasted forever.

"So what have we got?" Luke asked. "Since next week's meetings will be focusing on mid-August's shows, I'd like to wrap this up today."

"We've been reviewing storyboards," Susan said, answering Luke's question. "I like Cecile's ideas for the wives show a lot. They're great. I almost wish I could do them."

"Show me." Without taking a seat, Luke hovered while Susan displayed Cecile's work. "I like it," he said.

"She and I can switch segments," Cecile said. "I'm really curious about this fan stuff. I love sports—don't get me wrong—but I'd never buy acetaminophen just because a Bears or a Cubs player was on the box. I'm definitely interested in researching what makes these people tick so that Allegra can interview some of them."

"Well, switching wasn't what I was thinking, but we can definitely do that if you both agree that you want that," Luke said. "Consider it done. Here's our schedule. Research put together a list of fans who scored highest on the online survey on Allegra's Web site. Saturday I want those fans narrowed down to the few Allegra will interview on-site at the Brickyard. As for the driver segment a week from next Wednesday, I met with Ricky earlier and that's covered. Matt, you know what he wants you to do, right?"

"Yeah," Matt said. "I've got interviews and clearances already set up through the various PR people, track officials, NASCAR officials and the like."

"Super," Luke said. He'd gobbled down his sandwich. "Then I'll see all of you later tonight. I'm off to meet with Allegra to prep her on the afternoon shoot one final time. We had to change one of the guests at the last minute. He's too nervous to go onstage and broke out in hives."

And with that, Luke was gone, the only proof he'd been there was the wrapper he'd left in the trash can. Cecile didn't see him the rest of the day, although she did run into Allegra after the shooting wrapped when she stopped by the postproduction booth.

"Good to see you here, Cecile. How's your first week been?" Allegra asked.

Cecile shifted in her chair, pausing the feed of the final cut of next Tuesday's episode. "I've been studying the concept and I do believe I'm ready to do my first solo show."

"Luke says you are," Allegra said. The fifty-six-year-old was impeccably dressed, wearing the same yellow designer suit she'd worn earlier that afternoon. For the morning shoot she'd worn a blue dress during the interview with Elsa Tierney, a popular actress out promoting her latest action-adventure movie. "Luke's quite impressed with your work."

"Uh, thanks," Cecile said, flattered. "I've always wanted to work with someone like him. He's a great producer."

"I think so," Allegra said with a nod. "So tell me again what you're working on for next week," Allegra asked even though Cecile knew Allegra was always aware of what was going on with her crew.

But Cecile obliged, as someone who'd only been on the job four days would do. "I'm producing the segment that you're filming on Wednesday morning—on women who get themselves into the wrong relationships and how to get out. We've got five women lined up who will share their stories, and Dr. Lawrence will offer suggestions."

Dr. Henry Lawrence was Allegra's favored on-air psychologist. With a practice in Chicago, Dr. Lawrence appeared several times a month to offer counseling and self-help suggestions. He was always booked when the show involved relationships, like Allegra's once-a-month "Can this marriage be saved?" segment.

"Ah, Dr. Henry," Allegra said, glancing at the monitor Cecile had been watching. The show had been paused at the credits. "You'll like him. He's easy to work with."

"After that, I'm spearheading your back-to-school-week shows."

"That sounds great. Keep up the good work." And with that, Allegra was gone.

"Don't let her make you nervous," Gil said. He finished removing his headphones and grinned, his smile revealing two crooked front teeth. One of the best postproduction editors in the business, sixty-year-old Gil London was currently cutting together the Elsa segment with Ricky, who had stepped out of the room for a moment.

"Allegra likes to come scope things out," Gil continued. "Sorry I was present."

"It's fine," Cecile said. She knew if Allegra had anything bad to say she'd have done it in private.

Cecile pressed the button to restart her monitor's feed. "How long have you been working here?"

"Since she started ten years ago. Figured this was a chance to get out of Hollywood and settle closer to the grandchildren. Hate the cold winters, but the wife likes the Midwest and I love my wife. As for Allegra, she's finally starting to reach the place she wants to be. Of course, all this growth means she'll probably have to hire even more people. Not so much because of the way we film but just because each show is becoming more and more complex to produce. Nothing's simple anymore. Look at everyone having to go to the racetrack tonight."

Cecile shook her head. "I know. As soon as I get out of here, I'm on my way."

Gil laughed. "You hang in there. You'll do great."

"I'll try." When Cecile got back to her office, Janice was waiting for her. "What's up?" Cecile asked.

Janice handed over an envelope. "Here's your itinerary. Luke said he's made arrangements and will pick up your track credentials. Inside the envelope you'll find the track dress code. To go in certain areas you have to be wearing certain things, like long pants and closed-toe shoes."

"Thanks," Cecile said. She paused in her office doorway for a moment to study the package. Even though she knew little about stock car racing, she loved the thrill of being out on location.

As Joliet was about thirty miles southwest of the southern edge of downtown, Cecile calculated how long it would take her to get there. She'd need at least an hour and a half when factoring in rush hour, especially Friday night traffic. Then again, she also still had to go home and pack.

While technically the staff could have commuted to the racetrack for the weekend, staying on location eliminated the risk factor of transportation breaking down. In television production, a producer always considered every variable and worked to eliminate it. No one liked surprises. Cecile unfolded the reservation and studied it before glancing at her watch.

She walked the short distance to Janice's desk. "Janice, do I need to tell anyone if I cut out of here early and go home and get packed?"

"Just me. After you go, I'll field any calls and route them to your cell phone if necessary. You have Luke's cell phone number if you need it?"

"I've got it," Cecile said.

"Then you're good to go. Have fun."

Despite having done on-location shoots many times, Cecile found herself a bit nervous as she drove to Joliet later that night. She'd gotten a much later start than she'd wanted, for before she'd been able to leave the studio, one of the researchers had called her with a "quick" question about an upcoming show Cecile was producing and the subsequent conversation had lasted over an hour.

Traffic was heavy as Cecile left Chicago, and she wasn't surprised when she saw Luke's name on her cell phone's display about seven thirty.

"Hi, Luke. I'm on I-80 coming up on 30. I'm almost there."

"Great. I was wondering where you were." With that, Luke gave her his room number. "Have you eaten dinner?"

"I grabbed a candy bar and some Twinkies when I was getting gas."

"That doesn't sound like dinner food. Are you hungry?"

"A little," Cecile admitted as her stomach grumbled for emphasis.

"Then I'll order some appetizers for our meeting," Luke said. "See you in a few."

Cecile reached over and closed her phone. Within minutes she'd arrived at the Holiday Inn, gotten her room key and dropped off her carry-on bag. She took a moment to freshen up before heading up two floors to Luke's room.

Still wearing what she'd worn to work earlier that day, Cecile reached up and knocked. Luke opened the door and she stepped inside. Unlike her standard room, he was in a one-bedroom suite. She continued her way inside, noting the large work desk was already covered with his laptop, briefcase and files.

A small dining table had some covered dishes on it, and her stomach growled. The room service cart stood nearby, the fresh flower still on the linen as if it hadn't warranted being moved to the dining table. A quick view of the seating area showed that she was the only staff member present.

"Luke?" She turned around, facing him. He appeared a little haggard, as if he'd been running nonstop all day. Either that or he was nervous. However, that couldn't be it. She was positive Luke Shaw had never been nervous a day in his life. "Where's everyone else?" she asked.

"Out on the town," he said simply. "We met earlier. Since you were running behind, I told them not to wait. Most of them wanted to hit the casino."

"Karlene in Research called right before I left. She had some questions about the segment on women entrepreneurs."

"Are there problems?" he asked.

"No. She's just trying to narrow down the focus and wanted some clarification. Sorry I ran so late."

"It's no big deal. You've got a variety of shows on your docket right now besides this NASCAR one and you've done a great job balancing everything this week."

"So fill me in on what I missed," Cecile said, grateful for his understanding and his compliment. She crossed to the dining room table. The aroma of something delicious reached her nose, and her stomach grumbled hungrily. "Is this for me?"

"Yes," Luke said. "You said you were hungry and I'm a bit famished myself. I had to guess what you liked, so I hope it's satisfactory."

"I'm sure it's fine," Cecile said. One thing she wasn't was a picky eater.

"Good. Help yourself to whatever you want and feel free to raid what's in the refrigerator. There's beer, soda and bottled water."

"I've already had too much caffeine on the drive down here." Cecile removed a bottle of water from the refrigerator and began to lift the lids on the appetizers. Luke had ordered nachos and potato skins, which were two of her favorites. She served herself some of each and took a seat at the table.

"Those okay?" he asked, coming over and helping himself to a plate.

"Absolutely the right choices," Cecile said, taking a bite. She tried not to glance at him, for he wore shorts and a tight T-shirt that showed every sculpted muscle. She ate a potato skin and decided Luke should be forced to wear sack clothes. Something baggy. Anything to calm the electricity already humming underneath her skin and making her extremely charged. No wonder she'd tried so hard to avoid him this week. Now, alone in a room away from the studio, her hormones were revving into overdrive just from his proximity. He took a seat, and she managed to remain poker-faced as he took a bite, his lips opening and closing on the potato skin. Suddenly the only thing she felt hungry for was him.

"So what's up?" she asked, trying for a casual approach to hide racing nerves. After all, she'd been the one to choose option B, which was to focus totally on work, not him. "Tell me, what did I miss?"

HONESTLY HE WISHED she'd missed *him.* Luke swallowed the last bite of his food and exhaled slowly, drawing on reserve strength. The wise way to end an impossible week would not have been to have Cecile sitting in his hotel suite alone with him.

No one would ever mistake him for being wise, especially where she was concerned. While she might want to pretend the magical night they'd shared had never happened, he was finding that impossible. He wanted the first option. He wanted to indulge.

What he'd decided at the reception hadn't changed. Cecile was a woman he wanted to get to know, especially long-term. But she wanted all work and no play, which made him a very frustrated boy. At this moment, though, he had no choice but to oblige. Getting work out of the way was probably prudent.

"Tomorrow's pretty basic," he told her. "You'll go out and narrow down the list of fans Allegra should interview at the Brickyard. Just take notes as we won't be filming until Indy."

"That's fine," Cecile said. She'd finished some nachos and licked her fingertips. Luke gritted his teeth together and she frowned. "Anything else? You seem as if something's bothering you."

"It is," Luke admitted. Even talking about work wasn't diverting his attention. What he wanted was to draw Cecile into his arms and kiss her senseless. But she'd said no and he'd try to respect that. Even if it killed him. "I'm glad we're having this meeting. Cecile, you've done a great job this week. You've been professional and a breath of fresh air in production meetings. The show is benefiting from your presence."

"Wow, thank you," she said, a faint blush at his compliments flushing her cheeks. He held his breath for a moment. She had no idea the effect she caused. Luke had to admit he was beaten. Try as he might, this was no simple schoolboy crush. He didn't want to pressure her, but he had to get things off his chest.

"You're welcome for the compliment. You deserve it. But I have to be up front. I can't do this."

"Do what?" He could tell he'd lost her, for he knew she'd never seen him like this. Then again, he'd never been like this. Agitated from unrequited longing. He stood, food forgotten, and began to pace. He really did have too much energy.

He noticed she'd stopped eating and he moved closer.

Even from a few feet away she smelled like fresh flowers. And her hair. The fiery-colored strands that had charmed his fingers all night long during their love-making today hung loose around her shoulders. She was no angel, but she made a choir burst into song inside his head.

The heck with work. Some things in life were more important, bigger than the day-to-day. If a person didn't slow down and grasp what was in front of him, he might never have another chance. Was he the only one sensing what could be great between them? Was he the only one going crazy? Was he just a misguided, obsessed fool? He had to know.

"Have you thought about what you said to me that night?" he asked.

"When, after my sister's barbecue?"

He nodded. "Yes. Then. Do you know how impossible it's been for me to ignore you the past few days? To pretend we didn't share anything?" Luke asked.

"I—I suggested we try to get each other out of our system, but you turned me down. What else can we do?"

"One more night wouldn't have done it," Luke said, his tone rough. "I don't think there are enough nights."

"Oh," she said, those green eyes widening in surprise. "So have you reconsidered the options?"

"Luke, I…" she faltered.

He recklessly pressed on, not quite certain why, just that Cecile made him impulsive, made him fearless. "I can't stop thinking about you. Your body calls mine. Beyond the physical, your mind is in sync with mine. I look forward to hearing your ideas. I can't wait to spend time with you. I'm sounding quite pathetic here."

"Never," she said, her voice a whisper.

He raked a hand through his hair. "You've been staring at me all week. Glancing over when you don't think anyone will notice, especially me. Can you deny it?"

"No. But I didn't mean anything by it," she said.

But her expression betrayed her as she lowered her eyes and toyed with the linen napkin she'd placed in her lap. *Liar!* Luke thought triumphantly.

"Do you know what you do to me?" he asked.

She glanced up then, curious, more proof that her feelings ran deeper than she was letting on. He wasn't misguided. "No."

"None of my other coworkers make me want to rip off their clothes when they bump into me in an elevator," he said.

Cecile's mouth dropped slightly. She set down her fork. "Oh."

"Can you deny there's something here? Something more than just one night?"

"I can't," she admitted, the words squeaking out. She shook her head, strands of her hair dancing on her shoulders. "No, I can't."

He took her agreement as a positive sign. He sat in the chair next to hers, his hands planted on both knees as he faced her.

"If this is harassment, stop me now. Slap me. Tell me to go away."

But she didn't. She only watched his mouth as if remembering the way it had felt on hers. The nipping and the teasing. The tenderness.

"I wanted more after the reception, but the next morning you vanished without a trace," he said. "Next weekend we're supposed to go boating with your sister and Devon. How am I going to spend all that time with you and pretend I don't want you all to myself? I've tasted your skin. I've held your breasts in my hands. I've watched your face at the most intimate of moments."

Luke knew it was time to stop pussyfooting around the situation. Being this close to Cecile was killing him and it was time she knew it, if she didn't already. "Call Elizabeth and say I'm sick," she tried, but the words were quiet, and Luke knew she was caving.

He shook his head. "That won't solve the problem. I think it's best if we stop ignoring each other and explore this. I'm going crazy, but it's the good kind."

"You drive me crazy, as well," Cecile admitted quietly. "But Allegra. Our jobs."

"Yes," Luke agreed, doing his best not to grab her and kiss her senseless until he knew just how she felt. "You have to decide. I'm willing to risk it for you. This isn't playtime for me. This is real, and some things are worth the danger. You're worth it."

"I am?"

"Oh, yes," Luke said, realizing fully just how much he wanted her. He reached forward and traced her right cheek. "So worth it. And I want to show you exactly how much."

Chapter Ten

Upon hearing his words, Cecile froze. He'd practically asked permission, not simply taken action. The gesture spoke volumes. His lips beckoned mere inches from hers. He was her pied piper.

He was someone she couldn't resist. And why should she? She desired to taste his mouth at least once more. She wanted him inside her, wanted another moment of complete abandon.

He'd gotten under her skin, made her so prickly with awareness that she couldn't function. Deciding to ignore her feelings for him had been a desperate ploy for time. This moment had been almost preordained. So when he leaned over to kiss her, she whispered yes and kissed him right back.

Nothing had ever felt so right. And despite her worry about her job, Cecile knew she wasn't going to stop. At least not right away. Maybe not ever.

Kissing Luke felt like coming home. His lips on hers, it was just somehow fitting. She had to indulge. Taste. Savor.

She deepened the kiss, and he snaked his hands into her long hair, drawing her closer. "You are so divine," he whispered, and with those words she was lost.

They'd been in their own little world that night of the wedding and look where that had gotten them. Totally into this fine mess.

But as Luke kissed her, the magic returned. Her body reacted naturally, syncing into rhythm with his. Time, in a sense, stopped. Only the two of them were important in this moment. The rest of the details would work themselves out later. He'd said she was worth the risk. In her heart she knew that so was he.

His hotel bedroom was almost identical to hers. That was pretty much the last rational thought that registered in her brain before Luke's lovemaking swept Cecile away. Clothing flew and bodies merged. He kissed her everywhere, branding her as his, and she reveled in it.

If anything, this coupling was hotter than the one before, and finally she lay satiated in Luke's arms, the only glow in the room coming from the light slivering around the partially closed bathroom door.

"Satisfied?" Luke asked, cradling her close. She nuzzled against his chest. At this moment, everything seemed perfect.

"Yes and no. Yes, I'm satiated. But, no, I'm not sure I'll ever be satisfied. I don't think I'll ever not want more," Cecile said, her nose inhaling his delicious musky scent. "If anything, you're deeper beneath my skin."

"That's good to hear because that's where I like being," Luke said. He drew her closer and held her tighter.

"This is going to create all sorts of problems," Cecile said. "We work together, and I told you I'm no good with secrets. Did you know that I feel something akin to a spark of electricity whenever you're around? Yet I can't lose this job."

"And you won't," Luke soothed. "We'll keep things quiet. There won't be any awkwardness."

He stroked her hair, and Cecile could almost believe he had the power to make everything all okay. "Stop thinking about it," Luke commanded.

"I can't," Cecile said. "I'm like that. I process everything, usually after the fact. I wonder if…"

"It's worth it," Luke finished for her. "And it is. Where's that impulsive woman I met at the wedding, the one who met me barb for barb, jab for jab? The one who seemingly had no regrets?"

"She wasn't sleeping with her boss with her job on the line," Cecile said.

"So tell your close friends," Luke suggested. "Brag. Tell them you've got someone who satisfies you better than Bob."

"You *did* know what I meant!" Cecile said, her face pink as she remembered her conversation with Lisa.

"Of course I knew," Luke said. He stroked the tip of her nose. "I'll consider it an honorable duty to keep you from ever getting that desperate."

He was joking, but still she asked, "Do you always get what you want?"

She couldn't see his face in the darkness, but his words held firm conviction. "I told you that first night that I always have and always will," Luke said. "And I told you that I wanted you. I still do. I can't see that changing anytime soon, either."

He shifted, rolling her over onto her back so that he had her pinned. She could see pure intensity in his blue eyes. "In fact, I want you right now."

"Again?" Cecile said. The man had too much adrenaline, and she found it rubbing off on her. Like that first night, she was already good to go.

"Always," Luke said, lowering his mouth to kiss her. "Just remember two rules. One, I don't share. Ever. And two, just because we can't shout about how we feel from the rooftops doesn't mean I'm not craving you. I'll be aloof at work, but beneath my poker-face exterior know that you're driving me insane and that if I could, I'd bend you over my desk and show you exactly how much."

"I can handle those rules," Cecile said, because at this moment she'd agree to anything as long as it meant he'd keep kissing her. Raw happiness overtook her as his mouth laid claim to hers.

Maybe all would be okay. She'd waited a lifetime for someone like him. If he were her Mr. Right, he was worth the risk. The catch-22 was that she'd have to risk to find out if he was her "happily ever after." Incredibly, she found herself ready to do that.

"Love me," she told him, wrapping her arms around him.

"The best I can," Luke said as he began to make love to her again. "Let me show you how happy you make me."

And Cecile could only dream as she let herself be swept away.

LUKE HAD MEANT WHAT he'd said. Things went back to normal—or as normal as living with a secret could be— when everyone met in the suite's living area at eight the next morning.

Cecile had crept back to her own room at about five. She'd hated leaving Luke's bed, and when she'd tried to make her escape, he'd been awake and readily kissed her into submission, only allowing her to leave once he'd finished making love to her again.

She'd purposely arrived at the meeting a few minutes after everyone else, noting that the room service tray from the night before had been whisked away.

"Our goal is twofold," Luke said as he began the meeting. He gestured with his hands, and Cecile swallowed as she took a seat next to Susan. He had big yet proportionate hands that had loved her well.

"You look rested," Susan whispered. "I lost a hundred dollars last night. You were probably wise to have arrived late and avoided going to the casino."

"Probably," Cecile said with a smile as they hushed and focused on Luke's presentation.

Near the end of it, Luke paused and consulted his notes. "I'm scheduled to meet with tons of officials this morning, and Allegra's going to get to start the Brick-yard race."

"The gentlemen-start-your-engines part?" Susan asked. "I'm sure jealous."

"We all are," Ricky said.

"Anyway," Luke said, "I'll have all that nailed down after my meetings today. Allegra also mentioned that she might want to do some interviews with the NASCAR's head honchos. I'm hoping to finalize those this morning, as well. Cecile, you've got the infield campers. Those are the diehards, from what I understand. Here's a list of cell phone numbers and their locations in the field. Find them and pick one or two for our show."

"Got it," Cecile said. Luke continued to go around the room giving everyone their assignments. Pretty soon he had the meeting wrapped up and everyone was off, carpooling to the track in the two location vans. When they arrived, everyone except the drivers—who usually slept in—was starting to stir.

Cecile glanced down at the plastic pouch that held more track credentials that any human could possibly need. As she made her way to the infield RV camping, her phone rang.

She knew immediately who it was. "Yes?"

"Did I tell you that you looked great today?"

"No," she said, warmth spreading through her. She glanced around to make certain no one else could overhear the conversation. An elderly couple—who she figured were the Sanderses listed on her sheet—out reading books under their awning, stole a peek over.

"Well, you looked good enough to eat, so I might just have to taste you later…." Luke teased.

"Stop. Don't bother me," she replied. "You're distracting me."

Cecile noted that the couple had erected a flagpole, which was covered with flags of drivers' numbers; a picnic table, which was covered with a checkered table-cloth; and three blow-up palm trees. A barbecue pit stood near the door. The woman glanced over as if trying to read the credentials Cecile wore against her stomach. Cecile caught her eye and waved.

"So will I see you later?" Luke asked.

"Maybe when I'm not working," Cecile replied, her tone light. "I've found my first interview. Ciao."

She hit the jackpot immediately, deciding that Allegra had to interview the Sanderses, a married couple from Norman, Oklahoma. The Sanderses were lifelong fans, having traveled the circuit from before Rusty Wallace—their all-time favorite driver—was even a rookie.

"Ed used to race on dirt tracks," Jennifer Sanders said. "We made a bunch of friends over the years so there's a crowd of us. We always pull in together so we get camping spots next to one another," Jennifer added as Cecile wrapped up the preliminary interview. "We just tow our car and then, once we park the RV, we can drive to all the places not in walking distance. We've got paddock seats for the Brickyard."

"Right across from the scoring pylon and the tower," her husband, Ed, said. He was tall and beanpole-thin and he adjusted his baseball cap. "Since we're under the paddock penthouse, we're in the shade all race."

From there Cecile moved on, interviewing and nar-rowing her choices. The infield was like a small, energetic city, with traveling vendors selling ice and driver merchandise.

Around twelve-thirty her phone rang. It was Susan, who told her that some of the crew was gathering for lunch. As Cecile still had a few more people to scout, she declined. The race started at four, with prerace events before that, and she wanted to be finished before then. Once the race started, even talking about being on Allegra's show wouldn't be able to divert the die-hard fans.

She finished about three, but when she tried to call Susan, Luke and Ricky, no one responded. Her track credentials got her into the media area, but she'd gotten slightly grimy being out all day in the sun and she preferred not to wander into the media center and make less than a perfect impression.

So instead she explored a few merchandise tents, and when she walked past the Sanders' RV, they invited her to watch the race from the top of the vehicle. So she climbed up to watch some of the Busch Series race, and that's where Luke finally found her.

"Sorry for the confusion," he said. "Got your text messages."

"Did I mess up by not going to the media area?" Cecile asked, tilting up her sunglasses so she could see him better.

"No," Luke said. "The first van's gone. We're the last two still here aside from Ricky. He's a die-hard fan himself, so he wangled himself an invitation to watch the race from one of the driver's pits. Ricky said he'd make his way back later with the van, so you and I will get a cab back to the hotel and then we can head home."

"You should stay and watch the race with us," Ed said.

"That's very generous," Luke said. "Thanks."

Cecile smiled. "Can you believe how friendly everyone is? They see each other year after year at this race and keep in touch via e-mail. Thanks for letting me produce this show. I never realized the market for this stuff was so huge. Allegra's wise for tapping into it."

"She is, and I'm sorry we can't stay."

Cecile rose to her feet. "I know. Thanks for letting me hang out," she told the Sanderses. "We'll definitely be talking before the Brickyard."

The ride to the hotel didn't take long, and despite the desire flowing between them, Cecile and Luke held an animated conversation of the day's events. Even though they were alone in the cab, they were still on the job and thus refrained from giving in to what they really wanted, which was to kiss each other.

They'd checked out of the hotel before going to the track, so all Cecile had to do was retrieve her luggage from the bell captain and her car from the valet.

"Come home with me," Luke murmured. They stood in the lobby, appearing to anyone just like two friends or coworkers. "I'll follow you."

She had no plants or animals to care for. They'd had a successful day, and she wanted to see him. "Okay."

"See, we can do this," Luke said.

"We can," she said, longing to touch him.

But when they finally reached his condo, Luke paused when he reached for her.

"What?" she asked.

"You're sunburned," Luke said. "You're already quite red."

Cecile glanced down at her arm and pressed on it. Her red flesh temporarily went white, revealing a sharp contrast. "Oh, I am," she said, wincing. That was the thing about sunburn—you didn't feel it until way too late. "This is going to hurt later."

"Your face got it, too. I have some sunburn-relief gel in the bathroom. Let me get it and I'll rub it in for you. Have a seat. TV remote is on that table there."

"Okay," Cecile said, taking a seat. Instead of turning on the TV, she stared out the huge windows and closed her eyes.

SHE COULD HEAR someone calling her name, but her eyelids felt too heavy to even attempt to open them. After making love to Luke last night and then eating very little during the day, Cecile was wiped out.

"It's just me," Luke said as he settled beside her. He pressed something cold to her forehead.

"That feels good," she said.

"The aloe I brought will feel even better," Luke said. Cold gel hit her forearms, absorbed quickly by Luke's massaging touch. "Just lie still," he commanded as he spread the lotion over her arms. "I'm also going to have to put this on your face. You're as red as a beet."

"Lovely," she said, keeping her eyes wedged shut

against the light. The blackness somehow made the hurt bearable.

"I didn't even think about sunscreen," Luke said.

"You were inside all day," Cecile said.

"For the most part," he admitted. "I did go see some of the pits for a bit before the race."

His hands continued their gentle ministrations. "That feels so good," she said.

"So what was the best thing about your day," he asked, "minus the sunburn?"

"The Sanderses. They've been married almost forty-five years. Can you believe that? They were eighteen when they met and nineteen when they married."

"So do you want to get married?"

"Eventually," Cecile said. "Just not right now." The moment had gotten charged. Perhaps it was the administration of the aloe. Perhaps it was simply the way she was avoiding his gaze. To make light of the situation she joked, "Why? Are you asking?"

"And if I was?"

"You're funny," she said, sinking farther into the couch.

"I'm going to get you some water and acetaminophen. That'll help with the sunburn sting."

"You think of everything," she said, finally looking at him. Luke stood near her, silhouetted against the wall of windows.

"I try," he said.

And within seconds Luke was pressing acetaminophen into her hand and providing her with a glass of cold water with which to wash down the medicine.

She reached up and removed the damp cloth from her forehead before attempting to prop herself up on her elbows. "You shouldn't be babysitting me like this."

"I'm enjoying it," Luke said. "I care about you. What I feel for you is not all about getting you into bed. It's much more."

Cecile blinked and contemplated his words as Luke took the rag into the kitchen. Dealing with Mr. Right was foreign to her. She'd had a lot of Mr. Right Nows, but those hadn't been deep emotional connections. Although there had been friendship, she couldn't see any of them rubbing her with aloe just to make her feel better.

Cecile realized that in her previous relationships she'd always held something back. Perhaps it had been subconscious, but she'd refused to give all of herself, choosing to share only bits and pieces that she'd selected to reveal. She'd probably intentionally chosen the "wrong" man, because she knew she wasn't ready to settle down. Real relationships were scary. They involved trust. Emotions. They opened the heart to hurt, and who wanted to jump right in and risk that? Love didn't come with a safety net.

And now she'd found Luke, who, she realized, she was ready to step out onto a limb for. But he was her boss. As long as they worked for Allegra, they had to keep their relationship a secret. But Luke was worth the risk. Cecile finally understood what Tori meant when she'd said that loving your boss always changed things. Tori had been seeing Jeff Wright for years, and while her relationship was in a rut, she was correct in that the liaison had changed the office dynamic.

Eventually, if Luke did turn out *really* to be the one, Allegra would find out since Cecile would want more. If the relationship failed and things got ugly, Allegra would also find out. She was balancing on a tightrope in developing a relationship with Luke. The rush was exhilarating but also dangerous. If she fell, she'd lose it all and get hurt.

"Stop thinking about it," Luke said.

"What?"

"That you could lose your job," Luke said, reading her mind. "I won't let that happen. I promise you that. Don't push me away."

She wanted to question him as to how, but trust kept her from pressing. She instead simply accepted him at his word, which was a big step for her.

"I'll try. This is all very new to me. I've never dated a coworker."

"Neither have I," Luke said. "But life is too short to miss opportunities. If you want it all, you have to work for it. And you are absolutely worth fighting for. I've never met anyone like you."

He hadn't. And if he could simply get her to let down her defenses, the future was unlimited.

Heck, he'd even asked her to marry him. Well, sort of. That had been a test, his words more designed to find out if she planned to ever get married.

His actions proved how out of character he was behaving. They proved that she had more power over him than she knew. He had to handle the situation slowly and precisely, like negotiations between foreign countries. But that was hard. Cecile was the type of woman who could make a man want with only a smoldering glance. She wasn't a game player in the traditional sense. If he played hard-to-get and made her chase him, she'd opt out.

And he had much more to lose if it didn't work out. For Luke knew what Cecile didn't: that it wasn't really her job on the line. It was his. Allegra had made that perfectly clear in their conversation, and Luke knew Allegra well enough to know she meant exactly what she said. Friendship might be one thing, but business was business. But Luke kept all that to himself. He didn't want a relationship with Cecile built on misguided guilt—of her being worried about his career. He wanted her to fall in love with him because she wanted to, not because she had nothing to risk and felt obligated to be with him since he was willing to risk his reputation and career to be with her. He needed to be sure that Cecile wanted to be with him more than anything else.

They would simply have to keep their relationship to themselves for now. The corner of his lip inched up slightly as the irony struck him. Devon had described meeting Elizabeth as akin to being hit by lightning. Meeting Cecile had been more like being run over by a truck and then taken to the hospital via a roller-coaster ride. But, oddly, Luke wouldn't have it any other way.

Chapter Eleven

Cecile had finally returned to her apartment early Sunday evening around seven. Luke had insisted on caring for her, and she'd found herself not protesting or feeling restless and ready to flee. Luke somehow made her experience a sensation of being home, and they hadn't left his place, spending time Sunday watching DVDs from his expansive collection.

Because of her sunburn Luke had kept his hands to himself. Oh, she'd still wanted him—craved him, actually. But her tender skin had provided them a chance to retrench, to explore other aspects of their relationship. They'd simply been together as if on a first or second date, which had led to talking about all sorts of things from politics to favorite foods to vacations. Their conversations had run the full spectrum.

They'd discovered that they were extremely compatible in all areas, not just the physical ones.

Now home, she paced her small apartment, taking a moment to enjoy her city view. He'd held her all last night, rubbing aloe on her whenever she'd hurt. Never once had he asked for anything, even when he'd been pressed against her backside and she'd been able to feel his arousal.

She had no doubt that the next time they made love it would be cataclysmal.

Her cell rang, the tone indicating it to be one of her friends. She glanced at the display. "Hey, Tori."

"Hey. Called to check on you and to see if your apology worked."

"Haven't apologized yet," Cecile said. She'd forgotten all about that. After last night, she and Luke had moved beyond that point anyway.

"No? Then what's going on with you and Luke?" Tori asked.

"I think it's okay," Cecile said, taking a moment to fill her best friend in on the situation.

"Do you think you'll be able to handle this?" Tori asked once Cecile had spilled the weekend's events.

"No one's going to know," Cecile said. "Luke and I talked about that. Not seeing each other wasn't working. So we've decided to see what happens, but keep our relationship a secret. I mean, if this is the right man for me, I have to give it a shot, don't I?"

"Of course you do," Tori said.

Cecile sensed something underneath her tone. "What's going on?"

"Same old, different day," Tori said. "Work."

"Are you sure that's all it is?" Cecile knew Tori. Tori

was an open book most of the time, but when she had a secret, she guarded it closely.

"I'm sure that's all it is," Tori said. "I'm tired a lot, but my hours are longer now that I'm in management. Whoever said there was something as a forty-hour workweek lied."

"I've know that for years." Cecile had even worked on Christmas one year.

"Exactly. But I didn't," Tori said. "I've been spoiled, I suppose, and I haven't been sleeping well. The sun just comes up way too early, and I'm in a busy part of town. Constant honking and I'm not used to that. I'm going to look for a two-bedroom place out in the suburbs. Somewhere nice and quiet, even if it means a tad longer commute."

"Let me know," Cecile said.

"I will," Tori replied. "I'm glad things are working out between you two. And good luck tomorrow."

"Thanks," Cecile said.

She discovered she needed luck when she arrived at the office Monday morning, for working with Luke had suddenly become more and more difficult. And while she should have been happy that she could spend so much time with him, she found herself extremely agitated that she had to hide her feelings around her coworkers.

After all, Luke did exactly what she'd asked: he stayed away from her during work hours. During the eight o'clock production meeting he'd refrained from adding to the grief her coworkers dished out about her sunburn, but Luke's silence spoke volumes and had her remembering his aloe administrations. They'd felt superb, and his care had gotten her back on her feet much faster.

The brief daydream had made her flush, and Susan had leaned over and whispered conspiratorially in her ear. Cecile had quickly made something up that defused the situation before it spiraled out of control and she was reprimanded for her inattention.

She tried all day to focus for she had meeting after meeting, but she'd found herself acting like a school-girl with a crush. Watching Luke's fingers holding even something as mundane as a file folder reminded her of how his touch felt, all rough yet tender. His blue eyes had her remembering how his pupils would darken every time he looked at her.

Surely she was transparent and everyone around her could see her feelings and read her mind. But if so, no one said anything, and Cecile wrote off her irrationality as simple paranoia. She'd never be a successful criminal, that was certain.

So at five minutes to five she sat in her office, staring at the computer screen in front of her. She'd just finished typing e-mails approving scripts for two of her upcoming shows. She was to film her first segment on Wednesday.

Janice knocked on her doorway. "Do you need anything else? If not, I'm leaving."

"No, I'm fine," Cecile said, reading Tuesday's schedule. Tomorrow she had production meetings and also a budget meeting with the line producers for an upcoming show. Themed "Dress for success," the makeover show would feature real women in today's workforce. Allegra would hook them up with a fashion consultant, who would take them shopping for clothes. The goal was to help women dress professionally and tastefully so that they could get ahead in their careers, no matter what they were. Anyone selected got to keep the clothes purchased, so establishing the budget and keeping to it was crucial.

Cecile printed out a copy of her calendar, reached for the paper and heard a knock at her door.

"What did you forget?" she asked, turning to face Janice.

"I realized I'd forgotten to say hello and I wasn't leaving without saying goodbye," Luke said. He was lounging against the door frame, his body relaxed and casual.

Cecile reddened and glanced around to see who was about. Her blinds were wide-open and her office was near the elevator, so anyone going home would walk right by.

"Coworkers can pop in," Luke said, giving a plausible explanation for his presence.

She knew that's what everyone would think. But Cecile herself loved conspiracy theories. Her mind always looked for more details, suspected everything. She simply worked off the premise that everyone else working in journalism was like that.

"So what's up?" Cecile asked, going for the casual approach.

"I could ask you the same thing," Luke said. He

made no attempt to move. "Is your appointment at seven tonight?"

It took her a second to understand that he was wondering what time she was seeing him tonight. "Oh, yes," she said. "I have to go home first. It's going to last most of the evening, so I wanted to change."

"I hope you get some sleep," he said, somehow managing to keep the smirk from his face. He acted like a concerned boss, nothing more.

"Probably not," she said, folding her hands primly in her lap. Sunburn residual or not, she was touching him tonight. Period.

"Then I'll see you later," Luke said, the words nothing more than a generic goodbye if overheard by the chattering assistants who were waiting for the elevator. No one but Cecile understood the words' loaded meaning. Easing up, Luke stepped over to a group of women, said hello and disappeared into the elevator car with them.

Unaware she'd been holding her breath, Cecile exhaled. Maybe keeping this secret would become easier as the days went on. This was only the first workday they'd really been seeing each other officially.

She finished up the last of her work and about twenty minutes later headed home, gathered up some things, and went to Luke's.

He opened the door upon the first knock, as if he'd been waiting right inside the door from the moment she'd buzzed him from the lobby.

"Hi." She stepped inside and placed her tote and a small cooler on the floor.

"Hi," he replied, reaching for her and pulling her gently into his arms. "That doesn't hurt, does it?"

"No," she said. Any lingering sunburn discomfort was offset by the sensations his touch evoked.

"Sure?" he asked, his concern evident.

"The only thing that hurts is that you haven't kissed me yet," she said, reaching to bring his lips to hers.

"Happy to oblige," Luke murmured right before his mouth mated with hers. Cecile wound her hands into his hair, dragging him even closer. She wanted him inside her—now. They could have long and leisurely later, but the urgency had been building all day.

Frustration won out, and she removed her hands and went to work immediately on the button of his pants. His hands reached to still hers, but she pushed them away and tugged the zipper, kissing him all the while.

She caught his gasp of pleasure as her fingers found him through the gap in his boxers. She kicked off her flats, and together they coordinated their steps in a waddle that got them to the couch. Foreplay was unnecessary; she'd been tormented enough all day. His pants fell to his knees and she pushed him back on the couch.

She'd made one minor outfit change when she'd reached her apartment, shedding her work clothes for a short twill skirt and short-sleeve scoop-neck sweater. She'd come prepared and pulled out a packet from a front pocket. Luke's eyes widened but he made not one sound of protest.

She'd changed out her boring and basic lingerie, as

well, switching her regular cotton panties for a sexy thong. Unable to wait any longer, she rolled on the protection, pushed her G-string aside and impaled herself on his hard length.

A sigh of pleasure escaped her lips as she finally had him where she wanted him. He filled her, and she quivered as Luke tugged her shirt down, exposing her breasts to his waiting mouth. Cecile began to move, setting the pace, sending both of them quickly to completion.

Afterward she simply leaned against him, her body temporarily satiated. With Luke, once was never enough for her no matter how wonderful.

"I think I like this side of you," Luke said, his hands framing her face.

"What, the wanton woman?" she asked. They still hadn't pulled apart and he stirred slightly inside her.

Luke planted a kiss on her nose. "No, the take-charge woman who goes after what she wants. What man doesn't like to be greeted like that? Better than dinner any day. Although—" his stomach grumbled "—we will need to eat at some point. Shall we go out or stay in?"

"In," Cecile said, not ready to share him with anyone, even strangers. "I stopped and got some steaks. They're in the cooler."

"Then they're fine to wait a little longer," Luke said, reaching to remove her sweater.

"Yes," she confirmed and again let herself be swept away.

They made love, watched movies and finally Cecile

left for home around midnight. She slept soundly, and when she arrived at work the next morning, Luke again was hands-off and aloof. A pattern was quickly developing between them as they pretended not to know each other at the office and then met up at his place or hers at the end of the day.

"You look like you've settled in," Susan said as the producers presented Cecile with a celebratory cake after she finished filming her first episode.

"I think I have," Cecile said, even though she'd been working only less than two weeks. But she was becoming more comfortable with being highly aware of Luke's presence across the room. She constantly had him on her radar and knew he was the same way. The constant tingle she felt every time she saw him was starting to be easier to control. Now if only she could control the giddy smile that randomly crossed her face at any given moment, she'd be all set.

"Is that all it is?" Susan prodded. "To my female eye, you look like you're walking on air. New man?"

Oh, God, was it that obvious? "Sort of. We've known each other a while," Cecile said, tossing out a version of the truth. "He's a friend of my sister's. Things have just gotten more serious lately."

"I'm glad for you," Susan said, meaning it. Cecile felt bad about lying, but there was little else she could do. Susan had clearly picked up a vibe from her, and Cecile wondered again if her relationship with Luke was wise. She didn't want her secret exposed.

As for her first show, it made it through postproduction with very few changes and would air next Monday. Gil had declared the episode great, and Susan had told Cecile that was a rare compliment.

So, despite seeing her boss, by Friday she'd made it through her second workweek. Then the weekend came, which included the sailing date with her sister and Devon. She and Luke spent Friday and Saturday together, and at noon Sunday everyone met at the marina.

The day was gorgeous, the lake perfect for sailing. "So how are you and Luke doing?" Elizabeth asked. She and Cecile were in the galley, fixing a late lunch that they'd all eat up top.

"We're fine," Cecile said.

"Just fine? I've been watching him this past hour. He hasn't taken his eyes off you."

Trust Elizabeth to pry and matchmake. Would she be making a mistake telling her sister the truth? Cecile had been bursting to tell people about Luke but knew it could be risky. Telling Elizabeth, though, may give them something to talk about. "We're seeing each other but keeping it a secret," Cecile admitted, deciding that the truth *was* the best approach here. "I'm sure he's told Devon. Well, maybe he hasn't." Cecile wondered if that's what Luke might be talking to his best friend about right now. "Anyway, since we work together, the fewer people who know, the better, especially since Allegra frowns on fraternization and our dating could mean our jobs. I know I can trust you."

"Of course you can," Elizabeth said, clearly thrilled Cecile had confided in her. "And I'm happy you think that. It means a lot to me. I'm really glad you're back in Chicago."

"Me, too," Cecile said, realizing that this was probably the closest they'd ever gotten to expressing any real emotions. Growing up, they'd had little in common. They'd fought often, sure, at times yelling harsh things designed to hurt. But without either of them actually saying the words, they'd both just vowed to start anew.

"Are you two alive down there?" Devon called from the deck. "We guys are hungry and we've just found a perfect spot to anchor for a while."

"We're coming," Elizabeth said with a giggle. She made a face. "Men. Impatient about everything."

"That's for sure," Cecile agreed, and they carried the tray of food up the teak stairs.

She sat next to Luke, his presence welcome and yet a heated distraction as her body zinged every time he was inches away. The sensation showed no sign of ebbing no matter how much time she spent with him.

"Having fun?" he asked.

"Absolutely," she said, and the day ended too quickly for her liking.

"You know," Luke said as he drove her home, "you ought to give some thought to staying the night once in a while."

"I stay on the weekends," she said.

"I meant during the week," Luke said. "I hate that you have to leave. I'd rather hold you in my arms all night."

"I'd like that, too," Cecile said, "but it's not possible. We work together, and it's easier for me to get ready at my place. Besides, what if someone saw us come to work at the same time?"

"That's fine," Luke said, drawing her into his arms once they reached her apartment. "I understand."

But Cecile wondered about his acceptance later, and worse, his offer, especially when the thought kept popping into her head during the most inappropriate times throughout the week. She'd love to spend the night, but Susan kept questioning her, and Cecile knew the woman was only trying to be friendly. Normally Cecile wouldn't care and would share confidences. But this time she couldn't and the secret weighed on her mind.

She glanced at her watch, something she did a lot, as the workday schedule had to run precisely to the minute. At this moment, ushers were beginning to seat the afternoon audience.

Except for the first row of reserved seats, which were usually filled with relatives of show guests, most audience members who wrote in for tickets didn't know what show they would be seeing. Before each show a warm-up act kept the crowd entertained.

Occasionally, depending on the nature of the show, the segment's producer would also take the stage to prep the audience. Yesterday afternoon the segment being filmed had involved poverty and hunger, and Ricky had explained that some of the photographs shown might be graphic in nature and offered audience members a chance to leave.

Cecile had produced the morning show, a full-hour interview with an actress promoting her new film, which Allegra had previewed and loved. The actress had been on the show several times before, and this time Allegra had surprised her by finding her first drama teacher.

Today's afternoon show was about the NASCAR drivers. Ricky and Luke had been inside the greenroom for about fifteen minutes talking with the drivers and their guests, while Allegra was in her dressing room changing from the morning taping and redoing her makeup.

Although she normally would be busy with postproduction on the show she'd just filmed, Cecile was on the set so she could see firsthand the interviews given so that this show tied in with hers on NASCAR fans.

When Cecile heard she'd be working on a NASCAR episode, she'd asked if it was possible to get tickets to the taping for her friend Lisa. Luke's administrative assistant had come through with tickets for Lisa and her father, who happened to be a NASCAR fan, so Cecile's best friend would be in the audience.

Cecile tapped the headpiece woven through her hair. Since Ricky and Luke were busy with the guests, and she'd been too keyed up with Lisa and her father's arrival, Cecile had volunteered to do backstage duty, occasionally poking her head out around the corner of the curtain to see if her guests had been seated yet. They'd be in the front row, off stage left. The warm-up act would be onstage in about ten minutes.

"Everything in place?" Luke's voice said loud and clear, and Cecile jumped. He wasn't speaking over the audio link but rather standing directly behind her.

"It's all good," she said, his close presence flustering her the way it always did. Subconsciously he only had to stand near her for her body to short-circuit. "The director and the crew have just gone through their final checks and reported no problems."

Luke nodded. He'd be high in the control booth during the shooting, leaving Ricky on the floor with the director, who would oversee the cameramen and stage movement while Ricky oversaw everything else, including the filming schedule. While the final product would be only one hour long, taping would take about two to three hours.

"Has Lisa arrived?" Luke asked.

Cecile stole another glance. "Yes. I see her. She's just sitting down now."

"Great. Have someone tell her and her dad to remain seated once the show ends. I'll see if I can get her backstage to meet Allegra."

"That's so generous." Lisa's dad had been simply thrilled to be invited to a taping, and Cecile stared at Luke for a moment.

"Yep. That's me. Besides, I'll make you pay me back later."

"Uh-huh," Cecile said, turning her back so that she could maintain some composure at work. She knew exactly what Luke's innuendo meant.

"Just send them word," he said before disappearing.

So Cecile spoke into her headset, and within moments she saw a staffer relay the message. And then the warm-up act took the stage, and fifteen minutes later taping began.

"CECILE!" FROM WHERE she was being led backstage by a staff member, Cecile's best friend waved.

"Hi, Lisa! Thanks, Kara," Cecile said, relieving the assistant of her duty as the Meyer family approached. She gave Lisa a quick hug. "Okay, let me see."

Lisa held out her left hand, the diamond sparkling in the bright stage lights. "Wow. That's a rock," Cecile said.

"I know. It's a little ostentatious, but Mark insisted that he wanted the whole world to know I'm off the market. He's silly like that."

Cecile studied her friend. Lisa certainly appeared happy. In fact, her blond, blue-eyed sorority sister almost seemed to sparkle in a way that wasn't from the bright overhead lights that illuminated the stage.

"Well, welcome behind the scenes. How'd you like the show?"

"I can't wait to see it when it airs next week," Lisa's father, Mike, said. "I never realized so much work goes into making a show like this. Absolutely amazing. Thanks for having us."

"You're welcome," Cecile said. They wove their way through crew members who were already readying the set for the afternoon taping.

Lisa nodded. "I found it fascinating. I mean, as a political fund-raiser, I've had some of my clients be guests on talk shows, but I was always backstage. I never saw a taping from the audience. I didn't realize people simply sit and watch the commercials during the breaks. I thought those were put in later."

"It's all very complicated sometimes," Cecile said.

"There are so many little rules and regulations involving advertisers, crew breaks, etcetera."

"Well, I can't tell you how much my dad and I appreciate this," Lisa said.

"While we have to head back to St. Louis tonight, we do want to take you out to dinner. Are you going to be free to join us?" Mike asked.

"Actually, I was going to ask you both to join Cecile and me for dinner. That is, after you meet Allegra." Luke stood there, a smile on his face as he made his announcement.

"I'd love to meet Allegra," Lisa said, shocked at receiving the invitation crossing her face. Cecile knew the staff member who had asked Lisa and her dad to stay put hadn't told them why. "That's too kind, Mr...."

"Luke Shaw," he said, extending his hand, and Lisa shook it.

"Ah, so you're Luke. It's nice to meet you," Lisa said, her gaze speculative. Cecile averted her eyes. If you told one of the four Roses anything, you could assume they all knew. Cecile hadn't had a chance to talk with Lisa prior to her arrival, but of course Tori would have told Lisa about Cecile's "affair" with her sexy boss. Lisa would have also put two and two together from her phone call the day of Elizabeth's wedding.

As for the dinner invitation, she and Luke had talked about it yesterday. She just didn't think he was going to make it where anyone walking by could overhear. She'd planned to pull Lisa aside a little later.

But the two men were greeting each other and the group walked toward Allegra's dressing room.

"So that's him," Lisa said after pulling Cecile a few paces behind her father and Luke.

Cecile stopped short. "Shh. Talk in general. I'm dating a friend of my sister's. Remember?"

"Oh, okay," Lisa said, playing along. "This friend, he's a nice guy?"

"The best. I think I might be falling for him."

"Did I just hear you say what I think you said?" Lisa asked, but they'd reached Allegra's dressing room and were being invited inside, so Cecile couldn't answer.

Allegra's dressing room was actually a series of rooms. The first was a living area where she greeted her guests. Behind that were more rooms: her huge wardrobe closet, her hair and makeup room and her changing area.

Luke must have prepped Allegra for Cecile's friends' arrival, for she was waiting on one of the couches. She greeted Lisa and her father warmly, signed autographs for Lisa's mother and chatted for a few moments about Lisa's upcoming wedding and her work in politics before Luke ushered them out the door about ten minutes later.

"So dinner?" Lisa asked. "I'll ride with Cecile, if you don't mind, Dad."

"I'm sure you want to catch up on gossip," Mike said. "I've driven in Chicago before." And with that, the group was off.

"You didn't fly up here?" Cecile asked as both women closed their respective car doors.

"You know how Dad is. After being a pilot for years, he hates flying commercial. The plane he shares with his friend is actually undergoing some bodywork, so we drove. It was cheaper anyway, and the drive from St. Louis is easy. And stop trying to change the subject, which is that you didn't call me and tell me your news. He's gorgeous. He's got that glint in his eye, like how Mark used to look at me before I finally broke down and stopped fighting him at every opportunity."

"Luke and I don't fight," Cecile said, expertly weaving her way through Chicago's constant traffic.

"No, but you're still fighting him, aren't you?"

"What do you mean?" Cecile asked, taking a quick glance over at Lisa.

"I'm guessing you're fighting whatever feelings you have for him."

"When did you become a seer?"

Lisa smirked. "Ha, funny. Of course I know what you're going through because I went through it with Mark. When the right man comes along, he's scary. All your previous thoughts of how you'd handle it when 'the one' finally came along go right out the window and you're vulnerable. You and I lived together, Cecile. Deep down, I know you're very much afraid of failure, especially after Eric."

"Am not," Cecile protested, knowing that Lisa had hit the nail on the head. Cecile was afraid of failure, especially in the things that really mattered. She'd worked her whole life to get where she was in her career. She had a close circle of friends who supported her. But there was one area in which she didn't feel comfortable—love.

So she'd chosen men who couldn't get too close, those who she could handle and quickly put out of sight and out of mind. She'd fought off any deep emotional connection, building walls to protect her heart. When she thought Eric might have been the guy for her, she'd let her guard down and gotten hurt in the end.

"You love him, don't you?" Lisa asked.

"After three weeks?" Cecile said. "I said I might be falling for him, but I'm definitely not in love."

"See what I mean by fighting how you feel?" Lisa said.

"Hmm," Cecile said, refusing to answer right away. She found a parking lot, pulled in and paid the attendant. "Okay, fine, I'll admit this whole thing has put me in an awkward spot with Luke. I mean, he drives me crazy with the way he makes me feel. If he wasn't my boss, I'd probably be all over him and never want to come up for air. We went out on his sailboat with my sister and her husband last weekend and really enjoyed it. I'm always at his place or he's always at mine. It's like we're on a honeymoon where you never leave the hotel room. But eventually that's not going to be enough. Even though our relationship shows no sign of slowing down, I work with him. What are we supposed to do, get married and keep it a secret from everyone? I can't risk losing my job by shouting from the rooftops that he makes me happy. I want this job. I don't yet have enough experience to get a better position and I love what Allegra stands for. I do not want to go back to doing tawdry talk shows again. Why does there always have to be a catch?"

"I don't know," Lisa said. "But I believe that things always work out for the best."

"That's because for you they do. They always have, and I'm not trying to sound jealous or facetious with that statement. I'm not saying that life hasn't been rough in places, but for everyone who gets the brass ring, there has to be someone who doesn't. It's all physics. An equal and opposite reaction and all that. Maybe that's me," she said as she eased the car into a parking spot.

"Or maybe not. Maybe this is just one last challenge, a test. A hurdle."

The two women climbed out of the car and Cecile wrinkled her nose. "I usually like challenges. But not this one. I work with him. I'm already walking the tightrope and risking my job. That's too scary a possibility. How can I take this any further, even if—yes, I'll admit it—I do want more?"

"You take it further," Lisa said. "You just do." She saw Cecile's expression. "Oh, come on. Where's the girl who told me that *I* should go for it with Mark? You used those exact words last June. You told me I was stubborn. I'd say the pot's calling the kettle black here."

"But he's my boss. This is all it can be."

"You sound like Tori and I'm not buying that. Let me see if I can throw back at you some more of your words. Oh, *yes. He's gorgeous. He's a nice guy. Do you know how rare that is?*"

"I was describing Mark for you," Cecile said.

"And now I'm describing Luke," Lisa said smugly.

"So you just jump in. I have a feeling you think he's worth the risk if you've already gotten to this point."

"Do you know how much I hate you?" Cecile asked, beaten. Luke *was* worth the risk, but at the same time she was scared. She'd never felt so helpless. In the past, she'd always been prepared when it came time to end a relationship. But with Luke, none of the old rules applied.

"You hate me about as much as I hate you, sweetheart," Lisa teased. Having been roommates long ago and friends forever, she knew Cecile was just miffed at losing this argument. "So heed your own advice. If you like someone, you have to go for him. You can't miss an opportunity, even if he is your boss."

"Lisa, this is my career. I can't just start again. Surely you understand that."

"You know, I used to until I met Mark. Then I realized I could have everything I wanted, everything I ever dreamed of having, just like we toasted upon graduation."

"Well, I won't have anything if I get fired. Allegra told me no fraternizing. I've broken that rule multiple times, especially if you count what I did before I knew he was my boss. I might have had an excuse for that, but I don't have one now. Luke and I went into this eyes open."

"Speaking of," Lisa warned as Mike and Luke approached from their respective parking spots. "Do yourself a favor, though, and ask yourself what you are really afraid of."

"Being fired?" Cecile quipped.

"The Cecile I know was never afraid of anything.

Ever. She took what she wanted. I used to envy you for having that trait and wished I could be even a little like you. Don't disappoint me. I'm sure your fear is actually deeper than not wanting to go back to tacky television. Dig for it. When you do, you'll find your answers."

Everyone was getting the last word on her lately, Cecile thought as they entered the restaurant. Luke had phoned from the car, and they were seated immediately upstairs.

"So, Luke," Lisa said as appetizers arrived, "have you ever been to St. Louis?"

"Several times. Why?" Luke asked, scooping some nachos onto his plate.

"Because that's where I'm getting married," she said. "Mark and I finally set a date."

"You didn't tell me that," Cecile said. She took a sip of her wine. "When?"

"August twelfth."

Right around the corner, unless… "So next year?"

"Nope, this year," Lisa said, her expression dreamy. "We decided not to wait. We've been apart eight years and we're not wasting any more time. Mark's parents offered to hold the reception at their house. We'll set up tents in the backyard. And the wedding is going to be at Mark's local church."

Lisa had never been this impulsive. "But fittings and dresses and…" Cecile began.

Lisa took a sip of her water. "Mary Beth—Mark's mom—has some pull, and Neiman Marcus can have everything by our date without a problem. So all you'll need to do is go down to Michigan Avenue and have them measure you. As promised, the dresses I picked aren't ugly."

"You do have it all down," Cecile said. "Okay, count me in."

"I already have," Lisa said. "Plan on the Saturday before my bridal shower and then the wedding the next. Oh, and one more tiny detail."

Dread grew in the pit of Cecile's stomach. She knew that tone. "What?"

"You can't come stag like you usually do. This time, no matter what, Cecile, you have to bring a date."

Chapter Twelve

"Don't even think about it," Cecile said as Luke walked her to her car after dinner. Lisa and her dad had already left a few moments earlier, after saying their goodbyes and promising to stay in touch.

"What shouldn't I be thinking about?" Luke asked.

"The wedding. That she asked you to be my date," Cecile said.

"Oh, that. Well, you're wrong. You had no idea what I was thinking about. All I was thinking about was how you owe me a little payment for being so kind to your friends."

"I don't owe you a thing," she said.

Luke grinned. "No, but you'll pay up anyway because I make you feel so good when you do."

"You're impossible," Cecile said, annoyed that her body was already humming from his playful banter. "Lisa looked great, didn't she?"

"She looks happy," Luke said.

"She really is and it's wonderful," Cecile said. "We always thought she'd be the last of our group to get married. She never really dated anyone very long and was way too choosy. Now she'll be walking down the aisle in just a few weeks! Talk about a whirlwind."

"You think she's crazy for throwing together a wedding this fast," Luke observed.

"In a sense, yes. Not in a bad way, but when she first ran into Mark, she couldn't stand him. Now she's in love and ready to get married."

"It happens that way for some people," Luke said. "My parents describe their first date as spontaneous combustion. She wasn't wealthy. He wasn't poor. His family disapproved, so they eloped within three weeks and have been together ever since. My dad's parents weren't kind at first, but it was obvious she wasn't going anywhere despite their disapproval. For my dad, my mom was it. So my grandparents caved and came around."

"What choice did they have?"

"Exactly. See, there's that cynical nature I know and love."

"I'm practical," Cecile corrected. "I'm turning thirty three days after her wedding, and as I age, I become more practical and less gutsy. And she becomes gutsier and less practical. It's like we've switched personalities."

"It takes guts to do your job," Luke pointed out.

"Yeah, but that's instinct. I'm falling down in other areas."

"Like where?"

"Dating," Cecile said. "Tori's trying the online thing. Lisa reconnected with an old flame. And I…"

Am in love with my boss. Damn. Lisa had been right.

That's what Cecile had been afraid of all along. That when she finally fell in love, when she finally had it all, she wouldn't be able to keep it. She didn't subscribe to that "better to have loved and lost than never to have loved at all" theory. Cecile wanted her future to be assured, to be simple, clear and without fate giving her a nasty surprise around the next corner. But love didn't come with a guarantee.

"And you're what?" Luke prodded.

"And I'm stuck in a relationship that I have to keep secret," she said, grasping for something she could share. "I used to drive you crazy. You wanted me and couldn't have me. Now I have you. But keeping this a secret bothers me. And now I feel…"

Luke eased closer. "How?" he prompted.

"Well…" Now she'd done it. Opened her mouth and inserted her foot. She couldn't tell him she loved him. Not this soon. Not when she didn't quite believe it herself, and certainly not if she was the only one feeling the emotion. "Sometimes I worry this is all wrong," she said. That at least was the truth.

Luke stared at her a moment. "We are not a bad idea at all. We are very, very good together. I am extremely attracted to you, and as I said before, I don't see a slowdown anywhere in the near future. You and I connect on a lot of different levels. We're heading in the right direction."

Lisa's words resounded in her ear. *Go for it.* "We are," she said. "I don't want us to go backward, either. Perhaps, then, I should apologize for running out on you that first morning. It cheapened what we shared."

Luke stared at her for a moment. "You've been holding that in for a while."

"It never seemed the right time to say it," Cecile said. "But I guess I haven't moved past that morning yet, probably because I'm not often one to admit I'm wrong. But if we're going to make whatever this is between us work, then I'm willing to learn and to try."

"You are an amazing woman," Luke told her. "And your apology is accepted as long as you do some penance," Luke said.

"Penance?" Cecile wasn't sure whether she liked the sound of that.

But he was smiling, so she knew it was going to be okay. "Absolutely. You can start by stepping into my arms and kissing me."

A thrill shot through her. She'd missed his lips on hers. "We're in a parking lot."

"And you have something against a little public display of affection? Cecile, you can't live your life being afraid," Luke said, repeating what Lisa had said. "No one is going to see us," Luke continued. "Do you want to kiss me?"

"Yes," she said.

"Then kiss me." He reached forward and pulled her to him. "The only question tonight is, my place or yours?"

"Mine's closer," Cecile said automatically.

"Then there's your answer," Luke murmured as he brought his lips down to hers. The kiss was long and succulent, promising things to come.

"I want you, Cecile," Luke said when they parted.

"I'm going to that wedding with you as your date. I'm not planning on letting you go."

"Ever?" Cecile said, for his voice held a strange undercurrent.

"Not anywhere in the foreseeable future."

"That sounds serious," Cecile said, her mind frantically trying to process how this was all going to work out. Her body wanted his. Her mind needed him. Her heart...

Her heart was in love.

"I'm very serious," Luke said, drawing her even closer. "Let's go to your place and I'll prove exactly how much."

"Okay," Cecile said. "Lead the way."

"So how was your evening?" Susan asked Cecile when she arrived in the production room at 8 a.m. the next day. As was Susan's habit, she held a cup of coffee in her right hand. She claimed she needed at least three cups of java to get her moving.

"Great, why?" Cecile asked. She sat down and yawned. Maybe she should go get a cup herself; she hadn't gotten much sleep.

"You look tired," Susan remarked.

"Late night," Cecile said.

"So your friends liked the show and meeting Allegra?"

"They loved it," Cecile admitted. "Lisa's dad was in heaven. He got to see his favorite driver from the second row."

"Nice of Luke to get you those tickets," Susan remarked.

"Agreed," Cecile said.

"You should have had your boyfriend come watch, too," Susan said. "I'm sure Luke could have arranged it."

"Oh, he was working," Cecile lied. "He didn't mind. He's not really into NASCAR."

"What does he like?" Susan asked.

"Boating," Cecile said, reaching for a pen. "Fishing." A lot of guys liked that. Certainly she couldn't say sailing. Everyone at work knew about Luke's hobby; he had a picture of his boat in his office.

"So does your boyfriend have a boat?" Susan asked, but Cecile was luckily saved from replying as Ricky entered the room and began their meeting.

She opened the file folder he handed her. Cecile knew Susan was just being friendly since office coworkers frequently shared what was going on in their lives and the production staff here was no exception. Cecile knew all about Ricky's new grandson, Gil's upcoming trip to Cancun for his anniversary and Susan's mother's heart trouble.

But having to make distinctions between a fictional man and Luke was difficult. Cecile had actually found herself jotting notes to keep track of the white lies she'd told.

After the meeting she made her way back to her office. She bumped into Luke in the hallway, but as always, he simply said hello and passed by her as he headed to the studio for filming. He seemed much better at being able to keep the secret, darn him.

As for her, Cecile had discovered that she couldn't quite stay away from Luke at the office, and occasionally, he had slipped a kiss in now and then to her surprise. All they needed was one misstep and someone might see them. She hadn't encouraged his actions, though, because as exciting as being turned over his desk might sound, Cecile still worried that Allegra might find out about the relationship.

Already Susan was getting suspicious, and Cecile was running out of clever excuses as to why she wouldn't share her boyfriend's name.

Cecile sighed as she got back to work. In her world, when something seemed too perfect, it usually was. The other shoe had to drop at some point; it always did.

Or at least it had in the past. While Cecile wanted it all, her greatest fear was that deep down she really didn't necessarily believe that having it all was possible. Lisa had been right. Cecile's greatest fear wasn't about losing her job, but that perhaps the brass ring was meant for someone else.

She took a moment and stared around her office. She'd always been cynical and she'd grown more so over time. She'd produced too many television programs on human foibles to believe that happily ever after was a state that everyone reached. She was skeptical of the fairy-tale formula that sold greeting cards and flowers, and even if Lisa had found her prince, that didn't mean Cecile would. She was afraid she'd never have a love to end all loves.

Although that's exactly what Cecile wanted. That's why she kept trying, even after the mess with Eric. That's why she was risking everything for Luke. Love was like a lottery ticket—you couldn't win unless you played. If luck was with you, you just might win.

Cecile wanted to win, but she was tired of lies. Unless she left her job, though, which meant giving up and going somewhere less wonderful, she simply didn't see a solution except to keep the cover-up going. Somehow she made it through the rest of the workweek, although the dilemma remained when she saw Luke that weekend.

"What?" Luke said, drawing her into his arms. They were out on his boat, alone on a Saturday afternoon, anchored north of Chicago but not quite to Racine, Wisconsin. Next weekend they'd be in Indianapolis for the race, and having a free afternoon, they'd gone sailing just the two of them.

She shifted, the sheet sliding below her waist. "I'm just thinking," Cecile said.

"About what?" Luke said. They were below deck so he made no attempt to cover her exposed breasts, but instead smoothed her hair back from her face, his touch gentle.

"Just this. Us. Lisa's wedding."

"You think too much," Luke teased. He slid a finger across her cheek and tapped the end of her nose. "I'm always telling you that."

"Perhaps," Cecile said. "Lately I've been mulling things over a lot. Susan's really pressing for your name. I'm worried people are starting to get ideas about us. I'm thinking as much as I don't want to, maybe I should start looking for a new job."

"Do you want to do that?"

"No."

"Then don't. People always talk. The trick is to ignore

them. If they can't get the information they're fishing for, they'll move on to another pond," Luke said. He traced circles just below Cecile's collarbone. "I've made no secret of my feelings for you. Well, except at work."

"I know you care," Cecile began.

"Care?" Luke said. He straightened slightly and frowned as if her doubt troubled him greatly. "I do a lot more than care. You've become like a part of me. The best part, actually. I can't wait to get you alone at night. I want to be with you every morning. I want to wake up in your arms."

"Which, for the most part, you do," she pointed out. She'd begun staying over at his place more and more lately.

He nodded, a lock of blond hair falling across his forehead. "Exactly, we practically live with each other. Maybe we should officially move to that next step."

Cecile's heart clenched. While his declaration led in the direction she wanted to go, that same declaration had her applying the brakes.

Hindsight would probably have her wondering why she was bringing this up now, but it had to be done. "Luke, we've spent every waking moment together. How do we know that this is really right, that it's not something that will burn out? And living together didn't work out last time for me."

Luke's lips drew tight together before he spoke. "How about you just stop questioning everything? Let yourself be free to relax and be happy. Stop being afraid of the future, and I promise it will take care of itself."

"I'm trying," Cecile said. "I've even agreed to meet your parents."

"And that's a very good start. My mom's thrilled."

His touch was sweet torture, muddling her thoughts. He moved his fingertip lower.

"You're distracting me," she managed.

"I intend to."

"But I want it all, Luke."

"So do you want to get married?" he asked casually.

She stared at him, trying to read him. He'd asked that question once before in the same casual tone. She knew it wasn't a proposal. "You know I do. Eventually. We've had this conversation before."

"So stop being afraid. Let this develop naturally," Luke said, as if the solution were that simple.

"Now wait a minute." Cecile sat up quickly, her head almost banging against the wall. "Are you saying...?"

"No, of course not," Luke said with a sigh. "Cecile, words can't begin to express what I feel for you. Not when you don't believe."

He shifted and slid out of bed, leaving her abruptly.

She didn't appreciate his sudden cold shoulder. "You haven't even said you loved me," she told him. "And even if you had, it's way too soon for such declarations. We barely know each other."

Luke drew a deep breath. "We know each other in every way humanly possible. I'm going to check the instruments and the weather. There was a storm in the forecast and I want to make certain we don't get caught in anything."

He yanked on a pair of boxers and strode out of the bedroom. Cecile sat there for a moment, her anger growing.

She'd missed something. But this was ridiculous. You didn't make declarations of love after just a month of sharing a bed. Eric had done that and look how that turned out. She might feel as if Luke was the one, but she wasn't ready to risk tossing the words out there. She wasn't ready to go picking out china and crystal. Not that he'd really proposed anyway.

She balled her hands into fists and pounded her lap. He was so impossible! If only she didn't care about him so much.

But she did care. Greatly. She was in love with him. She paused. Love. Hadn't she just told him—heck, herself?—that it was too soon? Giving herself the out, she shook her head. What exactly was love, anyway? She'd thought she'd been in love once, but that hadn't worked out. Was love different each time? Or the same?

Love was not a raging river or an inferno that burned everything in sight. Cecile loved Luke, yes, but she certainly wasn't so besotted that she'd go jump off a cliff for him.

Not unless she were attached to a bungee cord, had received hours of instruction and had a safety net.

Her hand flew up to cover her eyes. She'd become like practical Lisa. Cecile had "gone for it," but this was as far as she was willing to go at this time. She wasn't ready to expose her heart again and risk getting hurt and possibly lose everything. She'd been through that once. This time she'd try the slow route. So right now she wasn't willing to move in with Luke, which meant giving up her apartment and her one-foot-out-the-door sense of freedom. She was happy being monogamous, but she certainly wasn't ready to close the door on her independence. She wasn't ready to risk having to uproot herself. Maybe in a few more months. When they were stronger as a couple.

Maybe then. She grabbed her things and began to dress.

LUKE CHECKED THE instruments and set a course back for Chicago. The weather forecasters had been correct, and a squall was coming in from the southwest. If they left now, they'd reach Chicago and be back at his apartment before the late-afternoon storm hit.

While the storm wasn't going to be anything too dangerous, it would make the lake rough, and Luke didn't want Cecile to be worried. He'd been through several squalls himself, and while he and Cecile would be fine, foul weather was nothing to be trifled with.

His grip firm on the wheel, Luke leaned back against the captain's chair. The boat sliced through the water easily, the diesel engines powering the sloop across the miles.

But as the bow cut through the water, Luke didn't necessarily experience the same elation he normally did. Usually sailing allowed him a chance to clear his mind, to simply be at peace out on the water. Even when racing against a storm, Luke never felt bereft, which was the only word to describe how he was feeling. He wanted Cecile. Unfortunately she wanted him, too, but not in the way he'd hoped. She was loving and giving in his arms. She made wild, passionate love to him that could only be described as soul-shattering. She was always ready for him and she was just as insatiable for him as he was for her.

But that was just physical need. Luke wanted more. He wanted her emotionally. To an extent, he could claim he had that, as he and Cecile had fantastic conversations that lasted into the wee hours of the morning. He'd never be bored listening to her ideas. He liked to hear her talk, enjoyed a good political argument.

But she hadn't told him her hopes and dreams, other than that she eventually wanted to get married and have it all. He assumed "it" was home, hearth, family and career, but he couldn't be certain. Most of all, Cecile hadn't shared her heart. For him, *that* was having it all: physical and emotional. He didn't want to settle for one out of two being "not bad."

For Luke, too, wanted it all. And he wanted that *all* with Cecile. She was the woman for him; he'd known it from the very first moment he'd laid eyes on her. Luke trusted his gut instinct, and Cecile had been like a blow to his solar plexus. Despite her challenging him at every turn, he remained totally convinced that she was the right woman for him. Nothing worth having came easy. She was like fine wine, needing nurture and care.

He loved her. He hated not telling her, not voicing the actual words, but doing so would probably send her packing, just as his offer to move in with him had. She wasn't emotionally ready to commit, although he knew she loved him. She'd erected walls around her heart to protect herself from her fears, fears that were very real to her. She might say she wanted it all, but for some reason, she was afraid of achieving it.

He knew the steps were going to have to be his. He believed in grabbing life's opportunities, and he wasn't going to lose Cecile. She loved her job, and he wanted her to stay with him out of love, not obligation.

"Are you okay up here?" Cecile asked. She'd arrived on the bridge.

"Storm's coming. Figured we'd go back, moor before the bad weather hits and maybe catch a movie tonight instead of staying out on the water until tomorrow like we'd originally planned."

"That would be okay," Cecile said. She stepped forward and gave him a kiss. "I'm sorry we were in a tiff."

"Nothing to be sorry about," he said, wrapping an arm around her and drawing her tight to his side, right into the space where she fit so perfectly. "All's well."

"Are you sure?" she asked, and he could hear her skepticism. He wished he could slay her dragons, destroy whatever had driven her to be so afraid of falling in love.

"I'm positive that all's okay," Luke said. He kissed her long and hard, as if to prove it to her. When he finally pulled back, she appeared a little shaken.

"Wow," she said softly. "You sure know how to raise my temperature."

"I hope I always will," Luke told her. The water was already starting to get a little choppy as the wind picked up. While the sky wasn't yet dark with storm clouds, the sun had vanished. He leaned over to give her another long kiss. "We'll be back soon. Do you mind straightening up below so we can get back to dry ground faster?"

"Sure," she said. "It's no problem."

Within seconds she disappeared. Luke could still picture her, standing there barefoot with her long strawberry-blond hair reaching the tops of her breasts. He could visualize the white cami top and the cutoff jeans that had emphasized her legs. But what had tugged at his heartstrings was that she'd come to make sure they were okay. Yes, this was a woman who loved him and probably didn't realize exactly how much. It was time he showed her.

Chapter Thirteen

The Nextel Cup and the Busch Series races weren't necessarily held at the same racetrack. Cecile hadn't learned that until later in the week, during the final production meeting before everyone left for Indianapolis for the Brickyard 400.

Cecile was discovering that, unlike baseball or hockey, NASCAR racing had way more rules and regulations. She could see how a fan simply couldn't learn overnight everything there was to know about pre- and post-racing inspections, the point systems, how to qualify and then driving and pit strategies.

"We'll have our tour bus just at the Brickyard," Luke told her and the on-site production crew during their final meeting. "Cecile, we're going to take a camera crew into whatever campground your interviews are at. Ricky, you're in charge of the shots of Allegra starting the race and any interviews afterward. She'll watch the race from one of the sky booths."

The group made final notes and adjourned for the

day. Studio filming was over for the week; from here forward crews would tape the on-site shows.

The crew was again staying in a local hotel, and the caravan of cars and tour bus arrived after midnight. Because the Brickyard race would host a quarter of a million fans and all the hotels in the area were sold out, all but Allegra and Luke were doubling up and sharing rooms. Cecile was with Susan.

"Come see me when you can?" Luke asked her during one quick private moment. But Cecile had no idea how they would manage that.

"I'll try," was all she'd said.

"You will," Luke had insisted, and as a thrill of danger had shot through her, that had been that.

Work called, and Cecile dedicated herself to doing her job. On Friday afternoon, two hours after Cecile had gotten everything at the campground ready, Allegra finally arrived on-site to begin interviewing the fans Cecile had screened at Chicagoland.

Then it was editing time, and she and her cameraman headed to the media area, where the bus was parked. She ran into Luke, who was approaching from the opposite direction.

"How'd it go?" Luke said.

"Great," Cecile said. "I've got all the footage I need. Jake did a great job."

Her cameraman nodded and climbed aboard the bus, leaving Luke and Cecile alone. "So are you editing right now?"

"Yes, Gil's already inside," Cecile said. "I'm determined to get this done tonight. Remember, I've got to get to St. Louis this weekend for Lisa's bridal shower. It's tomorrow night."

"When are you taking off?"

"Before noon tomorrow," Cecile said. "It'll take me at least five hours to get there. I appreciate you allowing Jake and I to finish up early. Lisa's rush sort of threw a wrench into everything."

"Not a problem. We'll handle everything. You do know, though, that I'm going to miss you," Luke said.

Cecile bent her head and glanced around. "I'll miss you, too," she whispered. "But I've got to be there for Lisa."

"As you should be," Luke said. "Let's get in there. Sooner we get done, the sooner we can spend a bit of time together before you leave for St. Louis." With that, they entered the bus. Once past the driver's seat, the first space was a living room and a small kitchen. The back of the bus held the editing suite and the recording studio. The bus also came equipped with satellite, which would be used to send the files to Allegra's studio in Chicago, where any final polish would be added on Monday.

They didn't break for dinner until well after nine o'clock when Cecile's segments were finished. After offering up his tape, Jake had left long ago and only Luke, Cecile and Gil worked to get everything edited. "Another great job," Gil said as he saved the last file.

"Thanks," Cecile said, grateful for his compliment. Her stomach rumbled; she hadn't eaten anything since a granola bar at two. "I'm famished. Luke? Gil? Anyone up to get some food?"

"I'm just going to have room service," Gil said as they left the bus and headed back to the hotel. "I want to lie down on my bed and stretch out. I've been in that chair most of the day. But thanks for the invite. You two have fun."

"Now we're finally alone," Luke said as the elevator whisked Gil away. They stood in the hotel lobby, looking from afar like two work colleagues saying goodbye. But goodbye was the furthest thing from either of their minds. "Room service sounds like a great idea," Luke said. "Come to my room for a while."

Cecile knew exactly where that would lead. "I'm rooming with Susan—"

"Who won't care when you get in," Luke said. "You're not keeping track of her, and she's not keeping track of you. So spend some time with me. I won't see you until late Sunday."

"Maybe even later," Cecile said. "I've got a luncheon on Sunday, so won't be leaving St. Louis until three."

"You should just fly," Luke said.

"Cheaper to drive, and I'm flying in for the wedding, using up my frequent-flier miles."

"So since you're not arriving home until late Sunday, stay with me now," Luke said. His hand on her arm spoke volumes, and Cecile stared at him a moment. Something in his expression was different this time. She could see urgency. Need. Desire. But yet, something more. Something she couldn't quite decipher.

She finally conceded, understanding that something more profound would happen tonight. Could he perhaps be developing deeper feelings for her? For all his joking about marriage, could he possibly be seeing her as the one?

Forgetting where she was, she shot her hand forward, taking his. "Let's go," she said.

His eyes darkened and he pressed the elevator button, his hand never disengaging from hers. They said few words, only expressing themselves through a series of gentle touches that grew more frantic once they reached Luke's room. Although they'd made love several times before, both sensed that this time was significantly different.

Wordlessly they'd crossed into a new place, taken their relationship to the next level. Their lovemaking was slow and sensual, growing like a fire from the smallest flame into something that burned both of them with desperate heat until the moment he drove himself into her and completed both of them.

She'd never been so whole. He was her other half and she loved him. Without thinking, she impulsively whispered the words into his ear, and he stilled, his body still engaged with hers.

For a moment she held her breath. Would the risk pay off? Had she made the right decision or said something that would make him pull back, panic and run?

He lifted himself then, moving so he could see her face. Resting his weight on one arm, he reached to touch her cheek with his free hand. "Those are the best words you've ever said to me. And I'm glad, for I feel the same way."

He dipped his mouth to take hers in a kiss that sent them spiraling, and she lost herself in the texture of his lips and tongue. He felt the same way she did, even though he hadn't said the exact words.

But it didn't matter. She could *feel* his answer in the way he held and touched her, as if she were a national treasure to be cherished and cared for. She experienced his sense of loss when she finally had to leave, drawing away from him to return to her room. The bedside clock had read three o'clock, and if she didn't get back to her room, Luke would never get any sleep. And he had to work tomorrow.

As quiet as a mouse, she inserted her passkey and sneaked back to her own room. She turned on only the hall light.

"You're in late," Susan said, the sound of the door opening having woken her up. She rolled over and blinked. "Did the editing last this long?"

"I overate at dinner so I decided to work out," Cecile said, still in the shadows.

"Oh, yeah, I forgot the fitness center here is always open," Susan said, her tone groggy. "I can't imagine ever thinking of working out this late."

Susan tossed an arm over her head and within seconds was back to sleep. Cecile forced herself to relax. There was a good probability that Susan wouldn't even remember the conversation in the morning or question her further. Besides, Cecile was leaving after breakfast. She got ready for bed and quickly fell asleep, a smile on her face as she remembered her night with Luke.

IT WAS ONE OF THOSE days, Luke decided the next afternoon. Physically spent from last night, Luke had pressed the snooze button on his alarm once more than he should have this morning. Then he'd nicked himself with his razor, making a tiny gash just below his chin. He'd skipped breakfast, grabbing only coffee. It was now close to one and his stomach ached. But hunger was the least of his problems.

The first NASCAR driver's wife to be interviewed had hated her hair and makeup, resulting in a huge delay as the stylist had had to redo everything. While Allegra wanted her guests to feel comfortable, any kind of delay put Luke's crews far behind schedule, throwing everyone off, including the wives and Allegra, who had commitments afterward.

Susan was frantically trying to shift everything around so she could make up for lost time. Allegra had taken the setbacks in stride, but Luke knew she wasn't happy. In the studio everything ran like a well-oiled machine. Even when it didn't, safeguards were in place to ensure minimal intrusion and disruption. On location, things could—and often did—go wrong. No matter how well organized, some events just didn't have contingency plans.

They finally finished shooting more than two hours later. Allegra's personal assistant had had to postpone Allegra's meeting with track officials, and Luke tried to mask his apprehension as his boss approached him.

They stood outside the last interviewed wife's motorcoach, and Luke knew that in the summer heat Allegra wasn't going to stay outside long, probably just long enough to express her disappointment in today's poor performance.

Even though some delays couldn't be helped, it was his job to see that problems didn't occur at all, so Luke immediately took the blame. "I want to apologize again for being off schedule," he said.

"It happens," Allegra said. "But perhaps you should have had more help so you could have run more crews. I thought Cecile and Jake were also part of this show?"

"No, only Susan and Ricky. Cecile and Jake were strictly the fan episode. They've already left, as planned."

"Giving us only two crews, which is why we ended up backed up. At Chicagoland you took four."

"Yes, because we were there for a shorter period," Luke admitted. "Budget came up with these numbers, and since Cecile's part was finished, I sent her on her way. And she had a bridal shower in St. Louis tonight which she'd requested to attend."

Allegra nodded. "Oh, yes. Her friend. Well, I'm hot and sticky and will need to freshen up before my next event. Let's talk more about this on Monday so we can avoid repeating problems like this in the future. Say about ten?"

"Ten," Luke repeated. He wasn't happy about this turn of events. But he knew Allegra. She would outline her displeasure and move on, so long as the problem was solved and never again repeated.

Still, the meeting wouldn't be painless. Luke's career was only as good as his last show. Start making too many mistakes, and he'd be out of work faster than a light flipped off at bedtime. He tried to put the thought out of his head as he headed back to his hotel room.

CECILE ARRIVED BACK in Chicago late Sunday evening.

She'd driven for hours through a thunderstorm that had stretched from just south of Springfield to just north of Joliet. The worst part had been that the storm had worsened, and she'd driven with white-knuckle tension as the rain and wind had pounded her car.

Luke had called several times, but she'd let the calls go to voice mail. It was close to nine before she dumped her suitcase just inside her front door, yawned and leaned back against the door for a moment. A long, hot soak in a bubble-filled tub sounded like exactly what she needed.

She'd been too busy with final dress fittings with her friends and a bridal shower to get much rest. She, Tori, Lisa and Joann had talked into the wee hours of the morning. While she'd loved spending the weekend with them, Cecile had realized she missed Luke.

While the bonds with her friends would never diminish, they'd evolved and changed. Joann and Lisa had each found their life's mate. No longer were the four dependent just on one another. They'd all fallen in love. Joann and Lisa had it all. Tori's love was unrequited. And Cecile was in limbo, unsure of what to do next.

Her phone rang again, and this time she dug into her pocket to answer it. "Hi, Luke. I'm finally back. I just got in the door."

"Good. I was worried. The weather's terrible."

"I know. I drove through it almost the whole way, and ironically it's starting to clear up now."

"Did you have a good time?"

Cecile eased up off the door and went to sit on her

couch. "I had a great weekend," she said as she proceeded to tell him about it. "How did the rest of the shoot go?"

"Fine," Luke said. "A few problems but nothing serious."

"That's good," Cecile said. She yawned again.

"You sound tired."

"I am," Cecile said. "I've missed you terribly, but if you don't mind, I'm going to call it a night and go to bed. I've got a production meeting at eight."

"Is this the teen makeover show?"

"Right," Cecile said.

"How about we have dinner tomorrow night?" Luke asked suddenly. "My place. I'll cook."

"Sold," Cecile said.

"Excellent. You get some rest, sweetheart, and I'll see you tomorrow."

She'd leaned her head back against the pillow and was in danger of falling asleep right then and there. "Tomorrow," she said. Luke was so understanding, such a rare quality in a man.

"Cecile?"

She had made the mistake of closing her eyes, the blackness comforting her like a soothing balm. "Hmm?"

"I love you," Luke said.

Cecile sat up, not sure if she'd heard him right. "What?" she said.

"I love you. I'd have told you in person tonight, but this will have to do. I'm not going another minute without saying it. Good night, darling." He disconnected, and suddenly Cecile was wide-awake. His tone had been serious.

He loved her. He'd said the three magic words without being prompted. Her entire body felt alive, giddy. Just maybe she was about to have it all.

WHILE IT MAY HAVE stopped raining outside by the next morning, inside things seemed to pour down. First a researcher called to inform Cecile that one of her upcoming guests wasn't quite who she said she was and that the background investigation discovered she'd been on several other talk shows, giving slightly different versions of her story each time. Cecile had immediately scratched her from the program and moved to one of the alternates. The change would require script adjustments.

Then she'd had a question about another show, on which she needed Ricky's help, but since he had worked the entire weekend at the Brickyard, he wouldn't be in until Wednesday. Already frustrated at the turn of events, she didn't immediately jump to happy thoughts when Janice popped her head in to say that Allegra's secretary had called and requested Cecile's presence in her office at two.

"Do I need to bring anything?" Cecile asked Janice.

Her assistant shrugged. "She didn't say, so just bring yourself. Allegra calls for last-minute meetings constantly. I'm sure it's nothing."

But Cecile wasn't so certain. Her gut instinct told her otherwise. Something was telling her that fickle fate had decided to drop the other shoe.

And why not? She and Luke hadn't been exactly private with their lives lately. She'd met his parents. She'd been out on the boat with Elizabeth and Devon. No one had asked them to keep Cecile's relationship to themselves.

Nervous about the meeting, Cecile tried Luke's extension and his cell phone, but she got voice mail both times. Not surprising since Luke was usually in nonstop meetings on Mondays. If he wasn't meeting with the producers in the afternoon, he was working with Publicity or with the line producers who managed the budget.

So promptly at two she found herself outside Allegra's office. "Allegra will see you now," the receptionist said, gesturing to the double doors, one of which was open. "Go on in."

So Cecile walked through and closed the heavy wooden door behind her.

Allegra was standing behind her huge mahogany desk, talking on the phone. "Yes, I'm handling it." She paused and gestured for Cecile to sit down in one of the chairs in front of the desk. As always, she was dressed perfectly, today in a designer business suit.

"No, I still don't like that idea." Another brief silence ensued as she listened to her caller. "No, not that either. My meeting just started. I'll call you back later." Allegra set the phone down and stood there a moment, glancing at Cecile as if studying her lime-green sweater set and dark blue pants. "Sorry about that," Allegra said.

"It's fine," Cecile said, her sixth sense off the chart. She sat on the edge of the chair and readied herself.

Allegra glanced at the clock. "I'm going to cut right to the point since I have another meeting in fifteen minutes. Cecile, you've done a fantastic job working for me. I'm thrilled I hired you."

"But," Cecile said for her.

"I know you're dating Luke," Allegra said flatly. "And I know you've been seeing him ever since you started working here."

Anyone's gut reaction would probably be to protest, but Cecile simply held herself still, especially since she knew Luke had told Allegra he and Cecile knew each other that first Monday.

"I've been able to ignore your relationship because up until this point it's pretty much been professional and kept away from the office. I asked Luke for that when he first told me about you two. But this weekend I had three camera crews at the Brickyard. When your segment was over, you left as scheduled."

Allegra shifted her weight and paused for a moment. "That mistake cost us valuable production time when we had some mix-ups. We could have moved you to the third location when the crew at location number one went overtime. I know mistakes are inevitable, but Luke was the one responsible for scheduling and for maintaining the budget. With your travel schedule the way it was, your show should have been transferred to someone else who could remain on-site in case we needed the extra people. It's a mistake we won't repeat the next time we film shows like this. I discussed this with Luke this morning."

"I understand," Cecile said.

"No, I don't think you do," Allegra said. "Nothing is textbook in this business and I've learned that many times. Whenever you think something is a sure thing, it still manages to backfire."

She tapped her manicured nail on the desk. "I want you and Luke to be a little more careful. I'm bending my policies a little for you two. After all, I am the boss and you both are excellent employees. So long as your actions don't interfere with the running of my studio again, I will have no problem. So far, minus this incident, you both have done a good job keeping your personal and professional lives separate. But this is a business, and if too many costly mistakes are made, some changes will have to be made, too."

"Of course they would," Cecile agreed. "I'm grateful that you are still giving me a chance."

Allegra smiled a little then, as if struck by a distant memory. "Who am I to stand in the way of happiness?" She became all business again. "So long as it doesn't interfere with my show."

"Thank you," Cecile said, standing when she sensed the meeting was over. She left the office, closing the door behind her. The click sounded like a deflating balloon. All the adrenaline whooshed out of her body and she slumped against the wall in the elevator.

She must be insane. She should be happy. Allegra had given her permission for Cecile and Luke to date, provided they kept everything professional while at work.

The meeting should have lifted her spirits, but instead

Cecile was melancholic. While Allegra had lightened her no-fraternization policy, she'd made it clear Cecile had compromised her professionalism. She should have remained at the Brickyard until all filming was finished, but she'd had Lisa's bridal party weekend to attend. Luke had known how important the weekend was to Cecile so he had let her go.

She shouldn't have put him in the situation. She should have reassigned her segment and given it to someone else who had the time to be there. Luke had considered her feelings, probably because they were dating. She'd put him in a terrible position.

And at what cost?

What would happen if she and Luke didn't work out? While Allegra hadn't said anything, Luke was the show runner, so surely he wasn't as expendable as she was. She would be the one needing to seek other employment. How many couples could work at the same place, and happily, anyway? Was this why she'd hesitated on moving in with him? He'd told her he loved her on the phone last night, yet she hadn't rushed right over to be in his arms.

"Meeting go okay?" Janice asked as Cecile returned.

"Fine. She had a question about an upcoming script and wanted to clarify a few things."

"Luke called while you were out. He'd heard about the casting change."

"I'll call him," Cecile said, heading into her office and closing the door. She needed to talk to him anyway.

He picked up on the first ring.

"I just had a meeting with Allegra," she began before her courage failed her.

"This sounds bad," Luke said. "Let me come down there." He hung up the phone and within moments was in her office. She swallowed as he twisted the blinds so they snapped closed.

He was dressed to the nines in a custom-tailored suit. "Allegra and I had lunch with some of our sponsors," he said, explaining his appearance. "What's wrong?"

"How come you let me leave the Brickyard if there wasn't anyone who could fill in for me? I don't want to be fired. My professionalism has been compromised."

"It's not your job on the line," Luke said. "It's mine. It's always been mine. I'm the boss. I made the mistake. That's what I told her."

Cecile shook her head. "Don't give me that. It's both of our problems. Why didn't you tell me Allegra had talked to you about this already?"

"You were tired. I figured I'd talk to you later tonight."

"And instead I walked into that meeting totally uninformed and unprepared."

Cecile leaned back against her desk chair. Luke had stayed standing, a powerful presence in her room. Her heart broke slightly. She did love him, but this wasn't going to work. Just as every man whom she'd thought was Mr. Right didn't work out for one reason or another.

She'd learned happiness was fleeting, so why would this time be any different? She could compromise in quite a few areas, but she refused to compromise her work ethic. That had been the one thing to sustain her all these years.

"I think I need to put some space in all this," she said. "This—us—has moved way too fast."

Luke appeared as if she'd physically slapped him. "You're not serious."

"I am," Cecile said. She'd never been more serious. "I need some time to think. I love you, but I don't know if I'm ready to risk all this. I don't know if I can stand losing my job. It's all I have."

"You have me," Luke said.

"That's not enough," Cecile said. "There's no guarantee this thing between us is going to work and I want it all, Luke. Everything." She bit her lip to keep the tears from flowing. She felt as if she was making the worst mistake of her life, but she couldn't stop it. In the end, she had to take care of herself and her survival. She had to protect her heart. "I'm sorry."

"No, I am," Luke said. He raked a hand through his hair. "I'm the one who's sorry. I believed in us. I wanted a future with you. You might be right. I think we both need to do some thinking. I'll catch up with you a little later, okay?"

No, not okay. She wanted him to fight. She wanted him to yell. To disagree. To make her change her mind. Anything. But fear kept her silent and she only nodded as Luke opened the door and walked away.

Chapter Fourteen

"What do you mean you told him you want to stop seeing him?" Lisa asked. She rattled the ice in her glass. "Things were going so great between you. How can you drop a bomb on us like this?"

"Easy," Cecile said, her voice shaky. "I just did."

Maybe she should have kept the secret to herself, but all her friends had been asking her when Luke would arrive in St. Louis and she just couldn't take the pressure.

The Roses—Joann, Lisa, Tori and Cecile—all sat inside the four-season room at Joann's parents' house. Since Lisa was marrying Joann's fraternal twin brother, the Smith household had become not only the location of the reception but also command central. Joann, Tori and Cecile were all staying at the house until they left Sunday.

The August day was hot, but the ceiling fans kept the air circulating and provided a comfortable breeze.

Lunch had been set on a rectangular white wicker dining table, which was covered with a bright red-and-white picnic-print tablecloth. Matching red napkins with white napkin rings and white china created a cozy cottage ambience.

"Please tell me you're making this up," Lisa said. She set the glass down. "Please do not tell me that you dumped your—"

"Boyfriend," Tori finished. She'd chopped her dark brown hair into a short, modern style that bounced around her chin as she talked.

"Exactly," Lisa said as she continued. "I can't believe you just gave up on him like that. I met him. He's the real deal."

"I haven't met him and even I agree he is," Joann said. She took a drink of her soda. Her own news had been that she was now expecting her fourth child, hopefully a girl to add to the mix of all boys in her household. Cecile studied her friend for a moment.

Joann was the petite one of the group, standing only five foot four. Funny how her brother, Lisa's fiancé, stood six foot one. Joann had dark hair and eyes and tiny bone structure compared to her friends. She'd barely shown at all during her pregnancies except for just a bump in the front.

Maternal instincts suddenly tugging, Cecile found herself hoping that someday she'd be so lucky as to look as great while pregnant. *Wait.* She'd just thought about having children. About wanting her own children. While she'd always assumed she'd have children, she'd never thought about herself being pregnant. Was it being with Luke all this time that was making her feel this way?

"Earth to Cecile. Did you hear us?" Joann asked. She snapped her fingers in Cecile's face.

"I heard you," Cecile lied.

"No, you didn't. We were asking if you loved him," Lisa said.

"I don't know," Cecile said, refocusing. "I think I do, but what is love?"

"Wonderful?" Lisa asked. "Exhilarating?"

"A husband who gets up in the middle of the night and drives to the twenty-four-hour convenience mart to get you ice cream?" Joann reminisced.

"One of you named a feeling and one of you named an action," Cecile said, trying to put the puzzle together now that the pressure was fully on her. She squirmed. "How do I know this thing between Luke and me is right? I can't be responsible for someone else. I barely can take care of me."

Lisa shrugged. "But what about the quiet times? Do you and Luke simply sit and be? Like when you're together and everything just seems like it's relaxed and perfect, no cares and no stresses?"

"Sometimes," Cecile admitted. "Normally that would bore me. I'd have one foot out the door so I could get going. But something about him makes me want to stay. I especially like being out on his boat with him, just out there on the water without any worries in the world."

"That's love," Joann said. "Sweetie, you've fallen, admit it."

"Is that why whatever this pressure is inside me hurts so much and is so scary?" Cecile asked.

"Yes," Lisa said with a sympathetic nod.

"Is that why our…?" Cecile flushed as she paused.

"Yes," Joann said with a laugh, lightening the moment. "That's why your lovemaking is so passion-ate. Why it's the best you've ever had. Why you can't imagine ever having another man in your life after him. Cecile, I've never seen you unable to talk about being with a man. You always regaled us with your stories. If you've suddenly gone mute, you must love this man. Luke—he's the one."

"I told you to hold on to him," Lisa said. She saw Cecile's stuck-out tongue. "Okay, so I told you to go for him. Same thing. Anyway, the bottom line is that you need to snag him up, not send him away."

"He probably hates me."

"He's not like Eric. Don't put words into Luke's mouth," Joann advised. "That's the first thing I learned about Kyle. Our brains work totally different. I think Kyle will react one way while in essence he reacts totally different from how I predicted. If you have a question, just ask Luke. Don't shut him down."

"Is he still coming to the wedding?" Tori asked. She'd been silent for a while and Cecile glanced over. She didn't seem as vivacious as she normally was but rather she appeared drawn and tired.

"Is Jeff escorting you?" Cecile asked, avoiding the question. She really had no idea if Luke was coming to the wedding. They hadn't talked since he'd left her office. Tuesday he'd been in meetings off-site. Wednesday he'd taken the day off. Thursday she'd left for St. Louis. So she'd just assumed that he wasn't coming and the answer was no.

"No," Tori said, her voice slightly strained. "I'm not taking Jeff. I'm going with one of Mark's groomsmen. Just as friends. We've already met. Trust me, there's no connection. Pity, for he's pretty hot."

"How's that Internet-dating thing going?" Lisa asked.

"Fine, but I'm so busy with work that it's been tough to date anyone more than once. And Jeff's a high standard to follow."

"You miss him," Cecile stated, sensing there was something more to this story.

"Yes and no," Tori said, her tone deliberately too light to ring true. She shrugged her shoulders. "Trust me, though, this isn't like you and Luke. You two really have something. Jeff sees me when it's convenient for him."

"He did say he loved me. I said I needed space. I hurt him," Cecile said, feeling terribly guilty.

"That's what happens sometimes," Lisa said. "Love's about give-and-take that's grounded in the best of intentions, but it's not always easy. Luke's made the first move. The next one is yours. The question is, what move are you going to make?"

"I don't know," Cecile said. "I mean, my job could be at stake. And working on *The Allegra Show* is such an opportunity." Cecile filled them in on what had happened.

"Cecile!" Joann seemed shocked.

"What?"

"You picked a job over a man? I mean, *the man?*"

Cecile stared at Joann. When her friend had discovered she was pregnant, she'd given up her career and married Kyle. They were very happy.

"You can always get a new job," Tori said. "I did."

"But it might be a step down," Cecile said.

"What's more important?" Lisa asked. "I had to learn that, too. A job is temporary. A husband is forever."

Cecile sat there a moment. They were right. She'd lost something more important. A career didn't keep you warm. Her friends had helped her remove the blinders fear had put over her eyes. She loved Luke. She wanted him forever.

"He joked around a few times about me marrying him. He wanted us to move in together," Cecile admitted.

"He did?" all three voices chorused. Her friends leaned forward.

"I told him no," Cecile said, explaining what had happened. Everyone seemed disappointed.

"You know, I think he's serious about this, about you. Maybe he was testing the waters, but no man mentions the word *marriage* at all unless he's thinking long-term."

"Maybe," Cecile conceded. "But what do I do?"

"We form a plan," Joann said. "Just like we used to do back in college. You know, we're still at a ninety-three percent success rate."

"I don't even want to remember what the seven percent failures were," Cecile said, adjusting her napkin.

"Nothing this serious, that's for sure," Joann said. "So a plan. Are we in agreement?"

"I think once they see each other, the wedding magic will simply take over again," Lisa said. "We need to make sure he's coming to the wedding. I'll take care of that."

"Sometimes fate helps you along and sometimes you have to help fate," Joann said. She glanced around at her friends. "This is one of those times. So before we start brainstorming exactly what to do, are we all in?"

"In," Tori said, moving her hand forward.

"In," Lisa said, placing hers on top of Tori's.

"You know I am," Joann said, putting her hand forward. They all turned to Cecile. "Well? Are you going to let four heads be better than one? Will you listen to our advice?"

Cecile sighed. Love was complicated, but if this was really it, she couldn't let it slip by. Not this time. She'd made so many mistakes already, and the week had been miserable. She'd tossed Luke aside because she'd been afraid. Well, no more. It was past time to show fate that she was the boss. She shoved her hand forward. "I'm in."

LISA REPORTED BACK the next day that Luke was coming to the wedding. When Cecile had pressed her on it, she'd simply said that the conversation had been very short but that Luke had agreed to do this one thing for her so that Cecile wouldn't be alone.

"I'm not a charity case," Cecile had protested, but Joann had told her that the goal was to get Luke to the wedding and that the ends justified the means.

Love was strange. It affected people differently. And the more Cecile thought about it, the more she realized she was very much in love with Luke Shaw.

Maybe it had taken her coming back to Chicago to shake off some of her New York pattern of simply being with a series of Mr. Right Nows. With Luke, she'd turned a page, started a new chapter in her life.

And she wanted Luke to be part of her future. She thought over the plan her friends had come up with. A bit untraditional, a return to the bolder, brasher Cecile. For the first time in a while she felt strong and confident, more like the woman who normally got what she wanted.

She refused to be afraid anymore. If the choice was her job or Luke, she was going to choose Luke. Jobs were fleeting and often temporary; she'd had several jobs since college. She only intended on marrying once, until death do us part.

After the Roses had knocked some sense into her, Cecile called Allegra Friday morning and let her know that if it came down to a choice between her job and Luke to let her know and Cecile would resign. Allegra had been stunned, and the conversation had been quick. Surprisingly, she hadn't been fired and still had her job come Monday. What she didn't have was her man.

So Luke had better watch out. For the first time in her life Cecile finally knew exactly, without one shred of doubt, who her Mr. Right was. And tonight she wasn't letting him get away.

Chapter Fifteen

He wasn't coming. As the clock inched its way toward five, she simply couldn't stand the anticipation. He had five minutes before she walked down the aisle—this time on no one's arm—and he wasn't there.

She glanced down at the pale pastel-green dress she wore. Lisa had held true to her word: the wedding party dresses were simple A-line sheaths that mimicked the classic style of Jacqueline Kennedy Onassis. They were gorgeous. The bridesmaids even wore white gloves that went two inches past the wrist and fastened with flat pearl-colored buttons.

None of that mattered if Luke wasn't here to see it. Cecile knew for certain he wasn't; she'd already poked her head out and wandered around the church. Several occasions she'd paced the main aisle, smiling at all the seated guests. The one and only time she needed a mimosa to calm down her nerves, the bridal party was holed up with nothing but water and soft drinks.

Tori had waved off champagne as part of her new

diet. Joann was pregnant. Lisa said she wanted to wait until after the event, which had been Cecile's philosophy up until this moment. She hadn't seen Luke since Monday. If absence made the heart grow fonder, hers was now about to explode from being so full.

He couldn't stand her up. He'd said he loved her. He'd told Lisa he'd be here. Maybe Cecile had hurt him far more than she'd thought.

"Cecile, it's time." Mary Beth—Mark and Joann's mom—gestured her over. "I'm about to walk down, so you need to get in your spot. Lisa's mom has already been seated."

"Will do," Cecile said. She put on a brave face and headed back to her friends. The groomsmen were already at the front of the church, having entered from the side. The ushers took Mary Beth down to her seat.

"Are you okay?" Joann asked. Being the shortest, she would walk down the aisle first.

"Fine," Cecile lied. She couldn't believe Luke wasn't here.

Lisa reached forward and squeezed Cecile's hand. "It really will be fine," she said. "Trust me. The plan will work. Now get down there."

Cecile didn't see how their scheme could work if he wasn't present, but she simply said, "Going," and got in line. The music started and Joann began her journey to the front. Tori followed, and Lisa's father stood nearby, ready to give his daughter away. He took Lisa's arm. Cecile sighed. She was next—and no Luke.

With a deep breath, she started down the aisle.

THIS HAD TO BE THE dumbest plan he'd ever considered, Luke thought as he slipped into the wedding ceremony the minute the bride had reached the altar and everyone had turned forward to face the minister.

But he'd agreed to do this Lisa's way, especially after she'd spilled how upset Cecile was and how much Cecile really cared. She'd winked at him from her place in the vestibule, spotting him where he'd been waiting in the wings just as they'd planned.

Cecile's friends had been quite the collaborators ever since Lisa had first called him. He'd been easy to find—she still had his assistant's phone number from her visit to the show. Luke sat in the last pew and wished he were closer so that he could see Cecile better.

She was radiant in that soft green color. She'd worn her hair up, and even from the back of the church he could see her long neck. If he played his cards right, he'd be able to plant kisses on that sweet expanse of skin for the rest of his life. He missed her, and had decided quickly that he'd been a fool for walking out of her office without a fight.

As Lisa and Mark said their vows, Luke found himself agreeing with every one. He'd love Cecile until death do they part, for better, for worse, for richer, for poorer. Hopefully all he needed was a little wedding magic, and from the collective sighs of all those in attendance when Lisa and Mark shared their first kiss as husband and wife, magic was definitely in the room.

Cecile didn't see him until after the ceremony, when she was walking down the aisle attached to the arm of the best man. Her green eyes widened when she saw

Luke, and he read the mixture of emotions that flashed there. Surprise. Anger. Relief.

He smiled at her and lifted his hand in a slight wave. The moment he reached the vestibule he took her arm.

"Hi," he said, sliding his arm around her. She stiffened slightly, but he wasn't to be dashed. "Get my message?"

"No," she said a bit noncommittally.

"I left you a voice mail," Luke said.

"I didn't get it."

He pulled her toward him, not caring who might see the gesture of affection. "Sorry I'm late. I didn't want you to worry. I had some last-minute business to take care of. I'll tell you about it later."

She fit next to his hip, and he liked it. "Are you going to kiss me hello?" he asked.

"I…"

He simply silenced her indecision with a long kiss. "I missed you, too," he said when they finally parted. "Do you have any wedding photos left to take?"

She shook her head. "Since Mark and Lisa already live together, we took them all before the wedding."

"I like your friends more and more," Luke said. "Smart people."

With that, he swept her off and directed her over to where her friends were standing.

There he met Tori and Joann. He met Joann's husband, Kyle, then a bunch of parents whose names he memorized so that he could place who went with who later. Then time for the reception.

"You and I need to talk later," she told him before

they separated. They would travel separately to the Smith estate.

But her words didn't worry him and he gave her a kiss on the nose. "Trust me. We're going to do a lot more than talk."

At Luke's loaded words, Cecile somehow managed a light, "Promises, promises."

Would she ever be able to read him? Maybe not. Maybe that's what kept the relationship hot and steamy and fresh. She'd never be bored with Luke.

His blue eyes darkened as his gaze held hers. "Trust me, we'll do a lot more."

As Joann claimed Cecile for the limo ride to the reception, Cecile found herself relieved but slightly shaken and giddy, too. His "more" comment had meant lovemaking, not fighting, yet they still had issues to work out before going further.

"So that's him," Tori said the moment she, too, climbed inside the limo's cool interior.

"That's him," Cecile said.

"He's hot," Tori said. "And definitely in love. You should see the way he looks at you. He can't take his eyes off you. So a sexy song, some wedding magic, and he'll be putty in your hands."

"I hope so," Cecile said. The plan was actually pretty simple. Lisa had worked a special song into the playlist for right after the bouquet toss. Cecile would catch the bouquet, dance with her man and then lead him aside and confess her love.

First, though, she knew she had to confront him

about their jobs and how they could make everything work. That wasn't part of the plan, but she didn't necessarily follow the Roses' directions to the letter. Certainly the night could end the way it had at Elizabeth's wedding, but that wouldn't solve their issues. On the dance floor Mark and Lisa were sharing their first dance. Now that dinner was over, Cecile knew she had to clear the air with Luke.

God had blessed Lisa and Mark, providing an evening temperature in the low seventies. Ceiling fans up in the top of the large party tent circulated the air, making the atmosphere perfectly palatable. A wooden dance floor had been erected, and Cecile skirted it as she went to where Luke was speaking with Lisa's dad. She approached, said hello and soon Mike Meyer left the conversation under the guise of finding his wife.

"What's wrong?" Luke asked.

"Nothing," Cecile said, her gaze sweeping the reception to determine the best escape route. "I just want you to myself."

"You're ready to talk now?" Luke said, reading the situation correctly.

"Yes, but not here," Cecile said. She held out her hand, and his touch molded to hers. "The Smiths have a koi pond back on the other side of those trees there. It's Mary Beth's retreat. She calls it her ten feet of paradise."

"I can see why," Luke said once they reached the secluded hideaway. Cecile led him to the curved stone bench that overlooked a lighted fishpond. The area was completely private, surrounded by five-foot floral hedges. Two solar lights illuminated a few footstones.

She sat on the bench, and Luke lowered himself next to her. "I discovered this place once when I was spending the night. No one will disturb us here."

"Good," Luke said, muddling her mind with a drugging kiss. His fingers slid into her hair.

"Later," Cecile said, pulling away. He'd tempted her all through dinner, but she couldn't falter. Not yet. "You and I. Talk."

"Yes, ma'am," Luke replied, mimicking her forceful tone.

"Seriously," Cecile said, and she was glad to see that Luke had sobered to attention. Not that he was drunk, by any means. He'd had one glass of champagne when toasting the bride and groom, same as she.

She took a deep breath. Her friends would have her seducing him right here, but secrets had gotten them into this mess and it was time all cards were on the table. "I called Allegra yesterday," Cecile began.

"You did?" Luke rubbed the satiny fabric that covered her thigh. She playfully slapped his hand away.

"Yes, I did," Cecile said. "I apologized for this week. I told her that I'm planning to go public with our relationship and that if she had a problem with it, to let me know so that I could start looking for another job."

Luke stilled. "You didn't."

"I did. I love you and I want you in my life. I'd like for us to be able to work together, but if not, I'm not going to put my life on hold out of fear."

A quiet fell as each of them took a moment to watch the fish swim in the pond below. She took a deep breath. "I can't live with myself if you lose your job because you're seeing me. We get along well. We love each other—or I think we do. You said it. I said it. We meant those words, didn't we?" Cecile shook her head, a few tendrils of hair falling from the updo.

"Of course we meant what we said." Luke took her hands in his and held her tightly. Then he loosened his grip and touched her left cheek with his right forefinger.

"I got impatient, didn't I?" Cecile asked. "I've ruined everything. I say no to going fast and then I'm the one moving at two hundred miles per hour. This certainly isn't the romantic moment I'd envisioned, but I'm going to try to keep muddling through and pray I don't make it worse. Luke, I've fallen in love with you. I don't do well with commitment. I'm terrible at it. I'm scared. I feel safe with you—until our jobs come into play."

"Cecile…"

"No, let me finish." She refused to botch things up any further. "I don't believe in fairy-tale hype. But I believe in us. I want everything to be good between us. Joann, Tori, Lisa and I hatched this plan the other day—"

"Lisa—"

"And I was going to present you with her bouquet after a slow dance, let the wedding magic take over and propose to you. Or accept one of your proposals. I believe that even though they were said in jest, you meant them."

"I did," Luke said. "But they weren't sweet or honorable enough. I should have had flowers, a ring… And I must tell you…"

She freed a hand and placed her fingers on his lips. "Luke, we met with wedding magic. I want our magic to last forever. I want to put things right. Marry me."

LUKE MADE CERTAIN not to wince. While he was beyond thrilled she wanted to marry him, he knew Cecile. She thought him innocent and he wasn't. He still had secrets he hadn't told her. The engagement ring Luke planned on offering Cecile sat like a weight in his left jacket pocket. As much as he would like to, he couldn't take the ring out, slide it on her finger and say yes to her proposal. He loved her, but they had to clear up a few final misunderstandings.

He had given Cecile space to miss him, but she wanted to marry him for the wrong reasons. She wanted to keep his job safe.

That was something she couldn't do, not when he knew something she didn't.

"Cecile, I love you," Luke said. He captured her gaze. "But we need to clear something up. Allegra called me to her office after you told her about us. You've pretty much vexed the woman. I've known her most of my life and have never seen her so flustered."

"What do you mean?" Cecile said. She bit her lip.

Luke knew he must tread carefully. He grabbed Cecile's hands so that she didn't escape at his next words. "Cecile, yesterday morning I told Allegra that I was going to marry you because I love you."

"She can't be taking this well."

Luke lifted her hands to her lips. "She didn't. She fired me."

Chapter Sixteen

"Fired you?" Cecile had managed to pull free and was standing now, her hair askew from the trembling that had consumed her body. "Because of me?"

"More or less," Luke said. "She gave me two weeks' notice."

"I thought you were off yesterday."

"No, I changed that. I took off Wednesday—because everyone should have an ace in the hole."

"An ace?"

He sighed. "After I put out some feelers, I received a call from another talk show in town and so I changed my work schedule around and took off Wednesday for the interview. They called to check my references Friday afternoon. That's when Allegra called me into another meeting. I didn't realize that you'd phoned her yourself already. No wonder she was panicking. She thought she was losing two producers."

Cecile's jaw dropped slightly. "You're willingly leaving *The Allegra Montana Show?* Why didn't you tell me earlier?"

"You'd broken our relationship off. If we were to be together, one of us had to leave. So I accepted the inter-view. I figured I'd tell you later. And, no, I'm not leaving the show. Allegra's first and foremost a businesswoman. I like working for her. I love working with you. I knew she'd fire me, but that was before she knew I was already headed to the competition. So she had to make some choices."

He stood and faced her but made no move to touch her. Instead he put his hand in his pocket. "She met my conditions and I'm staying."

"What conditions?"

"That she stay out of our relationship. That both of our jobs be secure. She's going to match their offer because, of course, she's not willing to lose two producers."

"And she agreed to all this?"

"She did. So I'm staying. We have no need to get engaged this fast just to save our jobs. They're safe. So we can slow this down, if that's still what you really want like you did before."

"I'm ready. I want it all. My offer stands." She jutted her chin forward.

"Then perhaps you need this." Luke withdrew a small black jeweler's box. "But we must clear up why I have this. I want you to be my wife because I love you with all my heart. And I've been stupid. I haven't said the words. I haven't asked properly. I've put feelers out, but I haven't been truly willing to risk exposing my heart because I thought you weren't ready. I was afraid of what you might say. Yeah, I'm big and bad, but I'd lost my heart to you that first night. If you said no when you believed I really meant it…"

He inhaled as if seeking strength to continue. "Cecile, you have walls erected deep inside you that keep you from having it all. But I want you. I want to spend my life with you, have babies and grow old together. I'm going to break all your walls down. If you'll let me. You and I, this is real."

Cecile sighed. "I agree. But even you have to admit this has all been very overwhelming."

"I agree. I fell in love with you at first sight. Do you know how cliché that sounds? Yet it happened, and I didn't know what to do. I wanted to jump right in, even if that meant I was gambling with my heart."

"You always get what you want."

"This time it was so much more than that," Luke said. "I saw my future with you. And, frankly, not having you in that future was simply unacceptable."

"Your future is with me," she said, her heart bursting, it was so full. "So what do you say? Shall we get married? Because I can't imagine my life without you in it, either."

He retrieved the box and flipped open the lid. "I've heard I'm a good catch."

"My friends think so," Cecile said.

"You've already stolen my heart," he added.

"You definitely have mine," Cecile said, snaking her fingers forward. "And that is a nice ring." The ring was a large emerald surrounded by diamonds.

"Green," Luke said, tempting her. "To match those

eyes I love looking into. Took me five stores to find exactly what I wanted."

"I do believe I would like to marry you," she said, her finger almost to the box.

He snapped the lid closed. "Only if we do this right," he said, his tone suddenly very serious.

She watched in loving awe as he dropped to one knee. The lights of the koi pond were soft, the water gurgling softly in the background. She could hear the strains of dance music, but that too faded away as he took her left hand in his.

She'd never seen such love or devotion, but it was there in the way he looked at her, and when he spoke, every word sent a thrill of happiness coursing through her.

"Cecile, you are the love of my life. Every one of those vows I witnessed today…I would like to make those vows with you. I love you. You are the one for me, and I can't imagine life without you. I would love for you to become my wife."

Wedding magic. It was real, and her heart over-flowed. She'd met him at a wedding, agreed to marry him at a wedding and soon she'd marry him at their own wedding.

"I love you, Luke. I may question this perfection we've created from time to time, for nothing in my life has ever been so fitting or right, and usually fate's not this kind. But you are the one for me and, yes, I'll marry you. I want nothing else but to be your wife."

"I love you, Cecile. So much." Luke rose to his feet

and dragged her into his arms. Their hands were a little shaky, but the diamond-and-emerald engagement ring slid onto her finger. And then his lips were on hers.

In the confines of the hiding place, she kissed him, until finally she drew back. "You're the only one I want from now until forever."

"Good," Luke said, his tone possessive. "Because from here on out, you're all mine."

"No, you're all *mine*," Cecile informed him, letting her ring catch the reflective light.

Luke gave her another long kiss. "You'll have no argument from me. Let the magic begin."

TORI KNEW SHE WAS probably the only one who noticed Cecile and Luke slip away from the reception after dinner. When she saw them later, Tori saw the flash of a ring on Cecile's finger as Cecile and Luke made a beeline for the house. Cecile waved her goodbyes and passed close enough that Tori saw Cecile mouth the cryptic words, *You're next.*

Then they vanished, headed to Luke's hotel, Tori surmised. That's where she'd go if she'd just said yes to the man of her dreams. She'd tell Lisa later that their plan had come to fruition.

Tori watched for a moment, happy for her friends. Mark and Lisa were busy wrapped in each other's arms, enjoying a moment alone before another guest claimed their attention. Joann and Kyle were dancing, taking pleasure in a night sans children. Kyle's hand often strayed to his wife's stomach, cherishing the new life growing there.

Taking a sip of her cola, Tori glanced around again. She was last. No man waited for her. Too bad she hadn't hit it off with any of her Internet dates. Not that she'd be dating anytime in the near future. She was getting a bit too heavy to date. She'd start to show very soon— a fact so far she'd been able to keep from her best friends. They were so wrapped up with Lisa's wedding, she didn't want to steal anyone's thunder with her own announcement.

She knew she should have told them this weekend that she was expecting and that, at this moment, she was planning on being a single mother. But she simply hadn't wanted to endure the endless questions. Yes, it was Jeff's. No, she hadn't told him. No, at this time she didn't plan on telling him. Tori was stubborn that way. Her friends would offer tons of unsolicited advice.

And she had her reasons for her secrets.

It wasn't as if he'd missed her since she'd moved to Kansas City.

Tori had only lasted in his life this long since she'd put up with the nonsense better than the rest.

But that was over. No more.

She stepped forward and stopped when a hand firmly grabbed her arm. Her cola sloshed, barely missing her dress as she jumped backward and held the glass straight out. Why, she ought to give the person a tongue-lashing for scaring her like this....

She turned.

"Hello, Tori," Jeff Wright said. "I thought it might be time we talked."

* * * * *

Will Tori find happiness with Jeff Wright?
Find out in NINE MONTHS' NOTICE,
the last installment of Michele Dunaway's
AMERICAN BEAUTIES *miniseries,*
coming from Harlequin American Romance
in April 2007.

Design Tip of the Day

Ambience is everything. Imagine eating a foie gras at a luncheonette counter or a side of coleslaw at Le Cirque. It's not a matter of food but one of atmosphere. Remember that when planning your dining room design.

    —Tips from *Teddi.com*

"Now that's the kind of man you should be looking for," my mother, the self-appointed keeper of my shelf-life stamp, says. She points with her fork at a man in the corner of the Steak-Out Restaurant, a dive I've just been hired to redecorate. Making this restaurant look four-star will be hard, but not half as hard as getting through lunch without strangling the woman across the table from me. "*He* would make a good husband."

"Oh, you can tell that from across the room?" I ask,

wondering how it is she can forget that when we had trouble getting rid of my last husband, she shot him. "Besides being ten minutes away from death if he actually eats all that steak, he's twenty years too old for me and—shallow woman that I am—twenty pounds too heavy. Besides, I am *so* not looking for another husband here. I'm looking to design a new image for this place, looking for some sense of ambience, some feeling, something I can build a proposal on for them."

My mother studies the man in the corner, tilting her head, the better to gauge his age, I suppose. I think she's grimacing, but with all the Botox and Restylane injected into that face, it's hard to tell. She takes another bite of her steak salad, chews slowly so that I don't miss the fact that the steak is a poor cut and tougher than it should be. "You're concentrating on the wrong kind of proposal," she says finally. "Just look at this place, Teddi. It's a dive. There are hardly any other diners. What does *that* tell you about the food?"

"That they cater to a dinner crowd and it's lunch-time," I tell her.

I don't know what I was thinking bringing her here with me. I suppose I thought it would be better than eating alone. There really are days when my common sense goes on vacation. Clearly, this is one of them. I mean, really, did I not resolve less than three weeks ago that I would not let my mother get to me anymore?

What good are New Year's resolutions, anyway?

Mario approaches the man's table and my mother studies him while they converse. Eventually Mario leaves the table with a huff, after which the diner glances up and meets my mother's gaze. I think she's smiling at him. That or she's got indigestion. They size each other up.

I concentrate on making sketches in my notebook and try to ignore the fact that my mother is flirting. At nearly seventy, she's developed an unhealthy interest in members of the opposite sex to whom she isn't married.

According to my father, who has broken the TMI rule and given me Too Much Information, she has no interest in sex with him. Better, I suppose, to be clued in on what they aren't doing in the bedroom than have to hear what they might be doing.

"He's not so old," my mother says, noticing that I have barely touched the Chinese chicken salad she warned me not to get. "He's got about as many years on you as you have on your little cop friend."

She does this to make me crazy. I know it, but it works all the same. "Drew Scoones is not my little 'friend.' He's a detective with whom I—"

"Screwed around," my mother says. I must look shocked, because my mother laughs at me and asks if I think she doesn't know the "lingo."

What I thought she didn't know was that Drew and I actually tangled in the sheets. And, since it's possible she's just fishing, I sidestep the issue and tell her that Drew is just a couple of years younger than me and that I don't need reminding. I dig into my salad with renewed vigor, determined to show my mother that

Chinese chicken salad in a steak place was not the stupid choice it's proving to be.

After a few more minutes of my picking at the wilted leaves on my plate, the man my mother has me nearly engaged to pays his bill and heads past us toward the back of the restaurant. I watch my mother take in his shoes, his suit and the diamond pinkie ring that seems to be cutting off the circulation in his little finger.

"Such nice hands," she says after the man is out of sight. "Manicured." She and I both stare at my hands. I have two popped acrylics that are being held on at weird angles by bandages. My cuticles are ragged and there's marker decorating my right hand from measuring carelessly when I did a drawing for a customer.

Twenty minutes later she's disappointed that he managed to leave the restaurant without our noticing. He will join the list of the ones I let get away. I will hear about him twenty years from now when—according to my mother—my children will be grown and I will still be single, living pathetically alone with several dogs and cats.

After my ex, that sounds good to me.

The waitress tells us that our meal has been taken care of by management. After thanking Mario, the owner, complimenting him on the wonderful meal and assuring him that once I have redecorated his place people will be flocking here in droves (I actually use those words and ignore my mother when she rolls her eyes), my mother and I head for the restroom.

My father—unfortunately not with us today—has the patience of a saint. He got it over the years of living with my mother. She, perhaps as a result, figures he has the patience for both of them, and feels justified having none. For her, no rules apply, and a little thing like a picture of a man on the door to a public restroom is certainly no barrier to using the john. In all fairness, it does seem silly to stand and wait for the ladies' room if no one is using the men's room.

Still, it's the idea that rules don't apply to her, signs don't apply to her, conventions don't apply to her. She knocks on the door to the men's room. When no one answers she gestures to me to go in ahead. I tell her that I can certainly wait for the ladies' room to be free and she shrugs and goes in herself.

Not a minute later there is a bloodcurdling scream from behind the men's room door.

"Mom!" I yell. "Are you all right?"

Mario comes running over, the waitress on his heels. Two customers head our way while my mother continues to scream.

I try the door, but it's locked. I yell for her to open it and she fumbles with the knob. When she finally manages to unlock and open it, she is white behind her two streaks of blush, but she is on her feet and appears shaken but not stirred.

"What happened?" I ask her. So do Mario and the waitress and the few customers who have migrated to the back of the place.

She points toward the bathroom .and I go in,

thinking it serves her right for using the men's room. But I see nothing amiss.

She gestures toward the stall, and, like any self-respecting and suspicious woman, I poke the door open with one finger, expecting the worst.

What I find is worse than the worst.

The husband my mother picked out for me is sitting on the toilet. His pants are puddled around his ankles, his hands are hanging at his sides. Pinned to his chest is some sort of Health Department certificate.

Oh, and there is a large, round, bloodless bullet hole between his eyes.

Four Nassau County police officers are securing the area, waiting for the detectives and crime scene personnel to show up. They are trying, though not very hard, to comfort my mother, who in another era would be considered to be suffering from the vapors. Less tactful in the twenty-first century, I'd say she was losing it. That is, if I didn't know her better, know she was milking it for everything it was worth.

My mother loves attention. As it begins to flag, she swoons and claims to feel faint. Despite four No Smoking signs, my mother insists it's all right for her to light up because, after all, she's in shock. Not to mention that signs, as we know, don't apply to her.

When asked not to smoke, she collapses mournfully in a chair and lets her head loll to the side, all without mussing her hair.

Eventually, the detectives show up to find the four patrolmen all circled around her, debating whether to administer CPR, smelling salts or simply call the paramedics. I, however, know just what will snap her to attention.

"Detective Scoones," I say loudly. My mother parts the sea of cops.

"We have to stop meeting like this," he says lightly to me, but I can feel him checking me over with his eyes, making sure I'm all right while pretending not to care.

"What have you got in those pants?" my mother asks him, coming to her feet and staring at his crotch accusingly. "*Baydar?* Everywhere we Bayers are, you turn up. You don't expect me to buy that this is a coincidence, I hope."

Drew tells my mother that it's nice to see her, too, and asks if it's his fault that her daughter seems to attract disasters.

Charming to be made to feel like the bearer of a plague.

He asks how I am.

"Just peachy," I tell him. "I seem to be making a habit of finding dead bodies, my mother is driving me crazy and the catering hall I booked two freakin' years ago for Dana's bat mitzvah has just been shut down by the Board of Health!"

"Glad to see your luck's finally changing," he says, giving me a quick squeeze around the shoulders before turning his attention to the patrolmen, asking what they've got, whether they've taken any statements, moved anything, all the sort of stuff you see on TV, without any of the drama. That is, if you don't count my mother's threats to faint every few minutes when she senses no one's paying attention to her.

Mario tells his waitstaff to bring everyone espresso, which I decline because I'm wired enough. Drew pulls him aside and a minute later I'm handed a cup of coffee that smells divinely of Kahlúa.

The man knows me well. Too well.

His partner, whom I've met once or twice, says he'll interview the kitchen staff. Drew asks Mario if he minds if he takes statements from the patrons first and gets to him and the waitstaff afterward.

"No, no," Mario tells him. "Do the patrons first." Drew raises his eyebrow at me like he wants to know if I get the double entendre. I try to look bored.

"What is it with you and murder victims?" he asks me when we sit down at a table in the corner.

I search them out so that I can see you again, I almost say, but I'm afraid it will sound desperate instead of sarcastic.

My mother, lighting up and daring him with a look to tell her not to, reminds him that *she* was the one to find the body.

Drew asks what happened *this time*. My mother tells him how the man in the john was "taken" with me, couldn't take his eyes off me and blatantly flirted with both of us. To his credit, Drew doesn't laugh, but his smirk is undeniable to the trained eye. And I've had my eye trained on him for nearly a year now.

"While he was noticing you," he asks me, "did *you* notice anything about him? Was he waiting for anyone? Watching for anything?"

I tell him that he didn't appear to be waiting or watching. That he made no phone calls, was fairly intent on eating and did, indeed, flirt with my mother. This last bit Drew takes with a grain of salt, which was the way it was intended.

"And he had a short conversation with Mario," I tell him. "I think he might have been unhappy with the food, though he didn't send it back."

Drew asks what makes me think he was dissatisfied, and I tell him that the discussion seemed acrimonious and that Mario looked distressed when he left the table. Drew makes a note and says he'll look into it and asks about anyone else in the restaurant. Did I see anyone who didn't seem to belong, anyone who was watching the victim, anyone looking suspicious?

"Besides my mother?" I ask him, and Mom huffs and blows her cigarette smoke in my direction.

I tell him that there were several deliveries, the kitchen staff going in and out the back door to grab a smoke. He stops me and asks what I was doing checking out the back door of the restaurant.

Proudly—because, while he was off forgetting me, dropping by only once in a while to say hi to Jesse, my son, or drop something by for one of my daughters that he thought they might like, I was getting on with my life—I tell him that I'm decorating the place.

He looks genuinely impressed. "Commercial customers? That's great," he says. Okay, that's what he *ought* to say. What he actually says is "Whatever pays the bills."

"Howard Rosen, the famous restaurant critic, got her the job," my mother says. "You met him—the good-looking, distinguished gentleman with the *real* job, something to be proud of. I guess you've never read his reviews in *Newsday*."

Drew, without missing a beat, tells her that Howard's reviews are on the top of his list, as soon as he learns how to read.

"I only meant—" my mother starts, but both of us assure her that we know just what she meant.

"So," Drew says. "Deliveries?"

I tell him that Mario would know better than I, but that I saw vegetables come in, maybe fish and linens.

"This is the second restaurant job Howard's got her," my mother tells Drew.

"At least she's getting *something* out of the relationship," he says.

"If he were here," my mother says, ignoring the insinuation, "he'd be comforting her instead of interrogating her. He'd be making sure we're both all right after such an ordeal."

"I'm sure he would," Drew agrees, then looks me in the eyes as if he's measuring my tolerance for shock. Quietly he adds, "But then maybe he doesn't know just what strong stuff your daughter's made of."

It's the closest thing to a tender moment I can expect from Drew Scoones. My mother breaks the spell. "She gets that from me," she says.

Both Drew and I take a minute, probably to pray that's all I inherited from her.

"I'm just trying to save you some time and effort," my mother tells him. "My money's on Howard."

Drew withers her with a look and mutters something that sounds suspiciously like "fool's gold." Then he excuses himself to go back to work.

I catch his sleeve and ask if it's all right for us to leave. He says sure, he knows where we live. I say goodbye to Mario. I assure him that I will have some sketches for him in a few days, all the while hoping that this murder doesn't cancel his redecorating plans. I need the money desperately, the alternative being borrowing from my parents and being strangled by the strings.

My mother is strangely quiet all the way to her house. She doesn't tell me what a loser Drew Scoones is—despite his good looks—and how I was obviously drooling over him. She doesn't ask me where Howard is taking me tonight or warn me not to tell my father about what happened because he will worry about us both and no doubt insist we see our respective psychiatrists.

She fidgets nervously, opening and closing her purse over and over again.

"You okay?" I ask her. After all, she's just found a dead man on the toilet...and tough as she is that's got to be upsetting.

When she doesn't answer me I pull over to the side of the road.

"Mom?" She refuses to meet my eyes. "You want me to take you to see Dr. Cohen?"

She looks out the window as if she's just realized we're

on Broadway in Woodmere. "Aren't we near Marvin's Jewelers?" she asks, pulling something out of her purse.

"What have you got, Mother?" I ask, prying open her fingers to find the murdered man's ring.

"It was on the sink," she says in answer to my dropped jaw. "I was going to get his name and address and have you return it to him so that he could ask you out. I thought it was a sign that the two of you were meant to be together."

"He's dead, Mom. You understand that, right?" I ask. You never can tell when my mother is fine and when she's in la-la land.

"Well, I didn't know that," she shouts at me. "Not at the time."

I ask why she didn't give it to Drew, realize that she wouldn't give Drew the time in a clock shop and add, "...or one of the other policemen?"

"For heaven's sake," she tells me. "The man is dead, Teddi, and I took his ring. How would that look?"

Before I can tell her it looks just the way it is, she pulls out a cigarette and threatens to light it.

"I mean, really," she says, shaking her head like it's my brains that are loose. "What does he need with it now?"

nocturne™

**WAS HE HER SAVIOR
OR HER NIGHTMARE?**

HAUNTED
LISA CHILDS

Years ago, Ariel and her sisters were separated for
their own protection. Now the man who vowed
revenge on her family has resumed the hunt, and
Ariel must warn her sisters before it's too late.
The closer she comes to finding them, the more
secretive her fiancé becomes. Can she trust the man
she plans to spend eternity with? Or has he been
waiting for the perfect moment to destroy her?

On sale December 2006.

SPECIAL EDITION™

**THE LOGAN FAMILY IS BACK
WITH SIX NEW STORIES.**

Beginning in January 2007 with

THE COUPLE
MOST LIKELY TO

by

LILIAN DARCY

Tragedy drove them apart. Reunited eighteen
years later, their attraction was once again
undeniable. But had time away changed
Jake Logan enough to let him face his fears
and commit to the woman he once loved?

REQUEST YOUR FREE BOOKS!
2 FREE NOVELS PLUS 2
FREE GIFTS!

American **ROMANCE®**

Heart, Home & Happiness!

YES! Please send me 2 FREE Harlequin American Romance® novels and my 2 FREE gifts. After receiving them, if I don't wish to receive any more books, I can return the shipping statement marked "cancel." If I don't cancel, I will receive 4 brand-new novels every month and be billed just $4.24 per book in the U.S., or $4.99 per book in Canada, plus 25¢ shipping and handling per book and applicable taxes, if any*. That's a savings of close to 15% off the cover price! I understand that accepting the 2 free books and gifts places me under no obligation to buy anything. I can always return a shipment and cancel at any time. Even if I never buy another book from Harlequin, the two free books and gifts are mine to keep forever.

154 HDN EEZK   354 HDN EEZV

Name _____ (PLEASE PRINT)

Address _____ Apt. #

City _____ State/Prov. _____ Zip/Postal Code

Signature (if under 18, a parent or guardian must sign)

Mail to the Harlequin Reader Service®:

IN U.S.A.	IN CANADA
P.O. Box 1867	P.O. Box 609
Buffalo, NY	Fort Erie, Ontario
14240-1867	L2A 5X3

Not valid to current Harlequin American Romance subscribers.

Want to try two free books from another line?
Call 1-800-873-8635 or visit www.morefreebooks.com.

* Terms and prices subject to change without notice. NY residents add applicable sales tax. Canadian residents will be charged applicable provincial taxes and GST. This offer is limited to one order per household. All orders subject to approval. Credit or debit balances in a customer's account(s) may be offset by any other outstanding balance owed by or to the customer. Please allow 4 to 6 weeks for delivery.

HAR06

HARLEQUIN®

American ROMANCE®

COMING NEXT MONTH

#1145 DADDY NEXT DOOR by Judy Christenberry
Dallas Duets

Nick Barry thought his new Dallas apartment was the perfect place to launch
his career...until he was bowled over by the trio of towheaded children next
door—and their gorgeous new mommy, Jennifer Carpenter. She had no time
for a man; besides, the hunk across the hall wouldn't want a ready-made family.
Too bad he was downright irresistible!

#1146 THE FAMILY RESCUE by Kara Lennox
Firehouse 59

After rookie firefighter Ethan Basque rescues Kathryn Holiday and her
seven-year-old daughter from a fire that burned down their home, he can't get
them out of his mind. He offers them a place to stay—but can Ethan convince
Kat he's not just trying to be a hero, and will be there for her always?

#1147 HER MILITARY MAN by Laura Marie Altom

Constance Price, aka Miss Manners, is at her wit's end when her boss wants
Garret Underwood, her biggest critic and the man she once loved, on her
radio program. Thankfully the navy SEAL is in town only temporarily.
Maybe Connie can save her show...and still keep their ten-year-old daughter's
existence a secret.

#1148 NELSON IN COMMAND by Marin Thomas
The McKade Brothers

Nelson McKade was a CEO—until his grandfather sent him to learn humility
at a dairy farm set to go "udders up." The power broker decided to play along
with farm owner Ellen Tanner's plan to save the day. But he also had a few
*un*businesslike moves in mind to get the gorgeous widow to see things *his* way.

www.eHarlequin.com

HARCNM1206